TRIAL BY
FIRE

TRIAL BY
FIRE

NORAH McCLINTOCK

ORCA BOOK PUBLISHERS

Library and Archives Canada Cataloguing in Publication

McClintock, Norah, author
Trial by fire / Norah McClintock.
(Riley Donovan)

Issued in print and electronic formats.
ISBN 978-1-4598-0936-9 (pbk.).—ISBN 978-1-4598-0938-3 (pdf).—
ISBN 978-1-4598-0937-6 (epub)

I. Title.
PS8575.C62T75 2016   jC813'.54   C2015-904528-2
C2015-904529-0

First published in the United States, 2016
Library of Congress Control Number: 2015946343

Summary: In this novel for teens, Riley gets a crash course in small-town
prejudice when an immigrant man is accused of a crime that Riley is
sure he did not commit.

*Orca Book Publishers is dedicated to preserving the environment and has
printed this book on Forest Stewardship Council® certified paper.*

Orca Book Publishers gratefully acknowledges the support for
its publishing programs provided by the following agencies:
the Government of Canada through the Canada Book Fund and the
Canada Council for the Arts, and the Province of British Columbia
through the BC Arts Council and the Book Publishing Tax Credit.

Cover design by Teresa Bubela
Cover photography by iStock.com

ORCA BOOK PUBLISHERS
www.orcabook.com

Printed and bound in Canada.

20 19 18 17 • 5 4 3 2

To Eli, for so many opportunities.

ONE

"Riley!" Aunt Ginny thundered. "Didn't I ask you to break down these boxes?"

I poked my head out the kitchen door and found Aunt Ginny in the middle of the veranda. Except for a narrow pathway from the door to the steps, it was filled with empty cardboard boxes and twists of newspaper that I had used to pack fragile items like dishes. In my defense, when it came time to move, I was the one who'd done the packing—all of it, including Aunt Ginny's bedroom, which, by definition, included Aunt Ginny's most personal items. She was too busy finishing up the paperwork on her open cases to help me. Then, when we got here, I did most of the unpacking. I hadn't got rid of the boxes yet, but it was on my list.

"Take care of it before I get back from work, will you?" Aunt Ginny said before trotting across the yard to her car. I surveyed the cardboard graveyard that was the back porch. It had never bothered me. I had spent most of my life moving around, especially when I was living with my dad's dad, my grandpa Jimmy, we were often on the road with his band. But then Jimmy died and I had to go to live with relatives I'd never even met. My mom died when I was a baby. My dad? He turned into Albert Schweitzer, and if you don't know who that is, maybe this is a good time to look it up. Dad's a medical doctor with an international charity, and he spends almost all of his time overseas, usually in places that are too dangerous for a kid. He spent a lot of time in Darfur. Now he's managed to get funding to set up a hospital in a remote area of Liberia. He emails me when he can.

Going to live with Aunt Ginny (my mom's sister) after Jimmy died was tough. But it was made a little easier by getting to know Grandpa Dan, Ginny's dad. The two of them, plus my uncles Ben and Vince, were just starting to feel like a real family to me when Aunt

Ginny got a job offer she felt she couldn't refuse, even though it meant another move for me, this time to a small town.

So now here we were, just the two of us, in a place where we knew no one and no one knew us.

Look on the bright side, Riley, I told myself. *There's always a bright side; it just isn't always what you expect.* That's what Jimmy used to say. One of the things anyway.

And there *was* a bright side.

My new room.

So when Aunt Ginny left, even though I'd intended to do what she'd asked, I decided the boxes could wait. Besides, the evening seemed to stretch endlessly ahead of me. There was plenty of time. I would break down the boxes and stack them neatly after I took another look at my room.

I loved it. It was huge—three times larger than Aunt Ginny's study in our old place, where I'd slept on a pullout bed for more than a year. My new room contained a brand-new actual double bed (with head- and footboards, a huge improvement over the creaky old hide-a-bed in Aunt Ginny's cramped second-bedroom-office) and offered a spectacular view of the rolling meadows and farmland surrounding the rambling Victorian farmhouse Aunt Ginny had rented. It also had high ceilings and gleaming hardwood floors. I was entranced by everything about it, except the color. The walls were a dull and grimy shade of off-white, like cream left out so long that it had crusted over. I'd cajoled Aunt Ginny into buying me some sunny-yellow paint. My plan was to start painting tonight. Maybe even finish painting tonight. Aunt Ginny wouldn't be back until morning. And it was summer. There was no school to get up for. I could paint until dawn, if I wanted to.

I pried the lid off one of the paint cans, dipped in a brush and applied a thick streak of yellow. It looked glorious, like the sun at noon, like daffodils, like summer. It didn't take long for me to forget about the boxes, and begin to transform my poor Cinderella walls into the fair maiden who steals the prince's heart. I didn't stop until I had finished one whole wall, and I paused then only because I was dripping with sweat despite the gentle breeze that I felt whenever I stepped in front of my open window. I was thirsty too. I went downstairs to get a drink.

I stood at the kitchen sink, gazing out the window while I ran the water until it got cold. There was an eerie brightness in the sky over Mr. Goran's place next door. I filled my glass and took it out onto the back porch to see what was going on.

Flames were shooting up into the sky over Mr. Goran's property. It looked like his barn was on fire.

I raced back into the kitchen, grabbed the phone and dialed 9-1-1. I reported what I had seen and gave the address and location as calmly as I could. "On Route 30, west of Moorebridge."

I slammed down the phone and raced outside again. Of all the places for a fire to break out, why did it have to be Mr. Goran's farm?

Mr. Goran! Was he home? Was he awake? Did he even know his barn was on fire? Was he out there now, trying to battle the blaze? Or was he frozen to the spot, flooded with memories and nightmares, unable to move?

I ran across the lawn, scrambled over the fence and raced toward the blaze, yelling Mr. Goran's name the whole way.

Lights were on in his house, but if he heard me shouting, he didn't answer. When I hammered on his front door, it swung open. I called him again.

No answer.

If the door was unlocked, that had to mean Mr. Goran was somewhere on the property. He had to be at the barn. I ran back to the barnyard and ground to a halt when I heard the scream. It was coming from the barn. I heard something else too. Banging.

"Mr. Goran?" I shouted. "Mr. Goran, where are you?"

"Help! Help me!"

The voice was coming from inside the barn. I raced to the door and tried to pull it open, but the latch handle had been heated to scorching by the fire. I yelped and yanked my hand back. It had been burned. I wound the bottom of my T-shirt around my other hand and tried again. The latch wouldn't give. It was stuck.

"Help!" Mr. Goran's voice was high and panicky.

I looked around wildly and saw a pitchfork leaning against the side of a shed. I could use it to pry the door open.

Whenever I think about what happened next, I see it as if I'm watching myself in a movie. I hear screams.

I'm halfway across the yard, focused on the barn and the flames and what I am about to do. I'm praying that I'll be able to do it because I know I'm Mr. Goran's only hope of escape. I run toward the barn. Then there is a deafening sound—an explosion—and pieces of wood and scraps of other things (I don't even know what they are) fly past me. Then something wallops me, and I am blown backward off my feet. It's a weird sensation. I see the barn getting farther from me instead of closer. When I land, the air is knocked out of me, and everything goes black.

I have no idea how long it is before I open my eyes. When I do, everything is blurry, but even so, I realize I am no longer alone. The yard is filled with people. One of them leans over me.

"Are you hurt?"

I try hard to focus. Why is this person shouting at me? And why does it sound like his voice is coming from the end of a long tunnel?

"Mr. Goran," I manage to say.

"I'm a firefighter. What's your name?"

"Did you get Mr. Goran out?"

"Mr. Goran? The owner?"

"Did he get out of the barn?"

Then someone else shouts. "There's someone in there!" At least, I think that's what he says. The voice sounds like it's coming from the next county. Everything gets blurrier and then fades to black again.

The next thing I know, someone is poking at me. I hear voices. Someone lifts me. I have a sensation of speed. Then nothing. Then bright lights and someone talking loudly, asking my name. More blurriness. More double vision. More blackness.

Then Aunt Ginny. And a massive headache.

"…concussion." That was the first word I heard when I woke up again. It didn't come from Aunt Ginny. It was spoken by a man, probably the doctor in the white coat I saw when I opened my eyes. He was talking to Aunt Ginny against the backdrop of a sunny window. I had slept the night away.

"We'd like to keep her here today," the doctor said. "When she goes home, she'll need to be monitored for a few days, just to make sure."

Just to make sure of what?

Aunt Ginny nodded. "I'll take care of it."

The doctor left, and Aunt Ginny sank onto a chair beside my bed. I'd never seen her look so worried.

"You're lucky to be alive, Riley," she said in a trembling voice. That surprised me. Aunt Ginny prided herself on being a strong person, and for the most part, that was exactly the image she conveyed. But she didn't sound so strong now. "Another inch or two and your head would have struck the corner of that cement." *Cement? What cement?*

"You could have died, Riley." Her face was pale. "What happened?"

"I was trying to get into the barn." I remembered that. But it was hard to recall anything else except why I was trying to get in there. I closed my eyes and tried to think. "There was an explosion. It blew me away like I was a piece of paper."

When I opened my eyes, Aunt Ginny's face was somber. And was that a tear gathering in the corner of her eye?

"I should have let you stay with Dan." She meant Grandpa Dan, her father, but she never referred to him that way. She never called him Dad or Father either.

It was a long story. "He's always around. You wouldn't have been alone. It's not too late to go back, Riley. School doesn't start for a couple of weeks."

"I'm fine, Aunt Ginny," I said, even though at that moment it felt like a gang of monkeys was playing Whack-a-Mole inside my skull. "I knew what I was doing when I said I wanted to come with you." Aunt Ginny had given me a choice: stay with Grandpa Dan and my uncles in the city, or move with her to the rural community where she had finally gotten a job as a police detective. "Mr. Goran was in the barn when I got there, Aunt Ginny. Is he okay?"

"He's upstairs, in Intensive Care. I'm not sure how he is."

"Can you find out? He was screaming." I shuddered when I remembered the terror in his voice. It was the most hideous sound I had ever heard. "He got locked in somehow."

Aunt Ginny frowned. "What do you mean, *locked in*?"

I struggled to recall. "The barn door closes from the outside with a latch. The latch was stuck. I was going to get something to try to pry it open with when the explosion happened."

"I'll look into it. But right now you need to rest. And I have to find someone to take care of you."

"I don't need taking care of. I'm fine." Except for the fact that suddenly I felt like throwing up.

"You have a concussion," Aunt Ginny said. "There's no way I'm leaving you on your own while I'm at work. What if something were to go wrong? What if you fell asleep and didn't wake up? What if you had a seizure or convulsions? What if…?"

"Aunt Ginny, you're scaring me."

"Good. That's why you need someone with you." She sounded like her old self again—brisk, in charge, matter-of-fact Aunt Ginny didn't believe in sugar-coating anything. Not at work or at home. "If anything had happened to you, you'd have been in for big trouble, young lady, and I mean it. Now get some rest. I'll be back in a while."

"Find out how Mr. Goran is," I called after her.

"Rest."

I tried to, but it wasn't easy. I kept hearing Mr. Goran's screams. And I couldn't shake Aunt Ginny's words. *Another inch or two…*

TWO

The next day they tested my memory, my balance and my coordination. And they warned me. Boy, did they warn me! *Take it easy. Don't do any strenuous physical activity. If anything feels off, tell someone. If your headaches come back, tell someone. If you feel dizzy, if you lose your balance, if you feel sadder than usual, if you…*

"What about Mr. Goran?" I asked the minute Aunt Ginny appeared. She had something behind her back, and I was curious about it. But first things first.

"What about *you*?" Aunt Ginny said. "How are you feeling?"

"That depends. Can I go home?"

"They're releasing you tomorrow morning." She produced an overnight bag with a great flourish and handed it to me. "I found someone to stay with you while I'm at work. She's also going to help get us unpacked."

I groaned and started to protest again. I felt fine.

"You either have someone staying with you while I'm at work, or I'll go and find that doctor again and make him keep you here."

Sometimes I could find a way around Aunt Ginny, and sometimes I couldn't. The stiff-jawed, sharply focused, cop-with-perp attitude she'd adopted as she insisted on a babysitter for me told me that she was dug in. There was no way she was going to budge, no matter what I said. I had no choice but to relent.

"Okay. But just for a few days, right?"

"Right," Aunt Ginny said. "Assuming you're okay."

I knew I would be. "So what's going on with Mr. Goran?"

Aunt Ginny's stern expression morphed into weariness, and she sank down onto the room's only chair. "He's in critical condition. He was badly burned, Riley."

"Is he going to be okay?"

She seemed to struggle before finding an answer. "They don't know."

That didn't sound good.

"I didn't do what you told me." I made myself spit out the words. I'd been thinking about them ever since I woke up. "You told me to clean up the porch, but I didn't do it."

"Clearly," she said. "I still can't remember what color the floor is." She peered at me. "What are you trying to tell me, Riley?"

"I started painting my room instead." But she already knew that too. How could she have failed to notice? She'd packed me a bag of clothes. "I only went downstairs because it was hot and I was thirsty. That's when I saw the fire. What if I hadn't been thirsty? What if there'd been a stronger breeze? I might not have gone downstairs at all. Mr. Goran might have burned to death in his barn."

I was shaking by then. I thought about my grandpa Jimmy. Boy, did I ever miss him! He wasn't the most educated guy in the world—he never finished high school—but he was one of the smartest. He read a lot and traveled a lot, and he knew more about how life worked than anyone I had ever met. Jimmy used to say that all of life, every single second of it, was balanced as if it were a penny about to fall one way or the other, heads or tails, fortune or folly, failure or success, door number one or door number two. He was so right. As soon as Aunt Ginny had left the house that night, I was that penny, and I'd fallen on the side of not doing what I'd been told to do.

Aunt Ginny shook her head. "They couldn't save the barn. They said that was obvious as soon as they arrived. After they got Mr. Goran out, they focused on making sure the fire didn't spread. They said barn fires are fast, especially in old places like Mr. Goran's, where the wooden barns have been standing for generations. It's quite possible that had you tidied up the porch and then gone upstairs afterwards, you wouldn't have seen the fire at all, certainly not from your bedroom. You wouldn't have been able to help."

It was nice of her to say that. But possible doesn't mean probable. Ever.

"What if you're wrong, Aunt Ginny? What if I'd seen it right from the beginning and called 9-1-1 right away? I was the only person who could have called. There's no one else close by."

"Mr. Goran is extremely lucky that you saw what was happening and called for help, that's for sure." She glanced at her watch and stood up. I knew what that meant. "The fire wasn't your fault, Riley. The fact that you happened to see it when you did? There's no doubt that's given him a fighting chance to live. And that's the end of the story as far as you're concerned. Now get some rest, and I'll pick you up tomorrow morning."

A small TV hung from a metal arm near the side of my bed. I reached for the remote on my bedside table and turned it on in time to catch the local news. I had to sit through the international stuff first, which I didn't mind. Jimmy had liked to keep up on world events, and I had sort of caught the bug. I wished sometimes that everything didn't sound so dire: another budget crisis, warlords and rebel groups in various countries in Africa (including the one where my father was), tensions with Russia, and the ongoing struggle between the West and extreme religious fundamentalism in the Middle East.

The network broadcast ended and a local anchor appeared to deliver the news closer to home: a proposed wind farm, which a lot of people were against; the shortage of school-bus drivers, which was going to be a huge issue in another month when school started; and rumors that a cannery in the area might be closing, which would eliminate a ready market for local farmers, who depended on the extra cash they received for selling their beans, peas, carrots and corn. Finally, there it was, news of the fire.

"Arson cause of Moorebridge barn fire," the pre-ad promo blared over a shot of the smoldering remains of the barn. I couldn't believe what I was seeing. I had been in that barn the afternoon of the fire. I'd gone over to tell Mr. Goran how terrific his salad veggies had been, and he'd shown me around. Now it was just a pile of burned-out beams and wet ash.

Six commercials later, a reporter shoved a micro-phone in the face of Fire Marshal Dave Brewster, who reported his finding that the Moorebridge barn fire had been deliberately set and that the matter was in the hands of the Moore County Police Service, where Aunt Ginny worked. I wondered if she was working the case. Even if she wasn't, she probably knew something about it. The reporter wrapped up by noting that the police were so far not commenting on the case.

I shut off the TV.

Arson.

Someone had deliberately set fire to Mr. Goran's barn. But who? And why his barn? He seemed like such a nice man. He was also our closest and only visible neighbor, which probably explained why he was the first to welcome us to our new house. He'd driven over in his red pickup truck as soon as the moving van had finished unloading everything Aunt Ginny and I owned. He'd brought us a basket of fruits and vegetables that he'd grown himself. He didn't stay, even though Aunt Ginny offered iced tea.

But he dropped by again first thing the next morning with flats of flowers and plants and spent the whole day grooming the overgrown flower beds at the front of the house and transplanting what he'd brought from his own garden. I went out and helped him. He spoke in a soft, accented voice. He was from Kurdistan, in Turkey, he said, where he had grown up on his father's grain farm. He told me all about life there—until Aunt Ginny called me inside.

"Here," she said, thrusting a small can of lighter fluid and a box of matches at me. "Go light the barbecue. I'm going to make hamburgers for lunch. It's too hot to cook inside. Besides, I can't find anything."

"*You're* going to make hamburgers?" I stared at her in disbelief.

"For your information, I do know how to cook."

Information? It was more like breaking news flash.

"Okay, okay," she said. "So I *sort of* know how to cook."

Who did she think she was kidding? Aunt Ginny knew how to open packages of food and heat up their contents. She knew how to boil water. She was quite capable of brewing coffee. But actually cooking?

"In other words," I said, "you know how to barbecue."

She did her best to look dignified when she said, "Yes."

Our barbecue was an ancient, kettle-like metal dome on skinny legs. It had been left by the previous tenant. I used the Jimmy method to light it: toss in some briquettes, squirt on some lighter fluid and throw a lit match on top of it all.

Flames shot up with a mighty *swoosh*. Mr. Goran turned at the sound and let out a shout, startling me. I jumped back involuntarily, bumping into the barbecue. It toppled over, strewing lit briquettes onto the dry brown grass at the edge of the patio. The grass burst into flames. Mr. Goran looked horror-stricken. He shouted in a language I didn't understand as I ran for the hose and doused the fire.

Mr. Goran's face had drained of color. His hand clutched his heart. His knees buckled. I turned off the hose and ran to grab him.

"Are you all right, Mr. Goran?"

He didn't seem to hear me. I led him to a lawn chair and sat him down.

"Are you hurt, Mr. Goran?"

"The fire." He was breathing heavily.

"I'm sorry. It was my fault. I should have checked that the barbecue wasn't so close to the edge of the patio."

"No, no, the fault is mine," he insisted. And then he told me about his father.

Mr. Goran's father had planned for Mr. Goran to take over the family farm one day, just as Mr. Goran's father had taken it over from his father. That plan changed in the late 1980s when war brought death and destruction to the region of Kurdistan where they lived. Mr. Goran's father was sympathetic to the rebels who were demanding an autonomous region for the Kurds. Because of that, government forces torched their farm. Mr. Goran's father died trying to save his few animals from the fire. Mr. Goran was badly burned. "I have scars on my back," he said. "Always I had nightmares, always about burning up." Mr. Goran's mother died soon after, a victim of starvation in the war that followed. Eventually the rebels were crushed. Mr. Goran and many others had to flee.

Aunt Ginny appeared with hamburger patties on a plate. She stopped short when she saw the barbecue, on its side on the burned grass and drenched in water, and turned to me for an explanation.

"Accident," I said. "Sorry. I'll have it ready to go again in a jiffy."

Mr. Goran stood well back, watching me nervously as I cleaned the barbecue and lit a new batch of briquettes. He didn't come anywhere near the patio for the rest of the time he was there. I had to take his lunch across the yard to him.

"Sorry," he said. "So sorry."

"It's my fault. I should have been more careful," I said.

I helped him finish the planting after lunch. While we worked, he told me it had been his dream ever since he'd arrived in Canada to rebuild what his father had prized the most—a family farm. It had taken a long time to make that dream come true.

"I worked two, three jobs at a time," he told me. "Every year, all the time, work, work, work. And now this." He swept a hand proudly toward the farm next door. "My own place." His only regret, he said, was that his wife had died before his dream came true.

We talked into the afternoon, working together and telling each other things about ourselves. When I asked if he had children, he looked troubled.

"A son," he said. "I am very worried about him."

Aunt Ginny appeared in a crisp lightweight suit. "Wish me luck. I'm off to meet my captain," she announced.

"Captain?" Mr. Goran looked confused. "You are in the army?"

"Police," Aunt Ginny said. "I'm a police officer."

Mr. Goran frowned. He finished up what he was doing and left soon after Aunt Ginny did.

And now someone had burned down his barn and, somehow, Mr. Goran had been trapped inside. It must have been terrifying for him.

Aunt Ginny didn't pick me up at the hospital the next morning. A stout, steely-haired woman who introduced herself as Stella Carter did. She bundled me into a wheelchair, telling me when I protested that it was hospital policy, and buckled me into the passenger seat of a hot-pink pickup truck with the words *Stella's Jams and Jellies* emblazoned on both sides.

"I brought you a couple of jars," she said.

She drove me home and made me lie down in the living room where the TV was in case I got bored.

I'm not sure when I fell asleep, but I did. Stella shook me awake.

"Just making sure you're okay," she said softly when I opened my eyes. "Feel free to drift off again."

The next time I woke up, the house was filled with the aroma of cooking, the table was set for supper, and Aunt Ginny was home again.

I waited until Stella left before I asked Aunt Ginny if she'd heard any news about Mr. Goran or the fire. I braced myself for her standard "I can't talk about an ongoing investigation" response.

But she didn't say that. Instead she said, "Mr. Goran's condition hasn't changed. But, Riley, I think you should know there's a suspect in the arson investigation. It's Mr. Goran."

"What do you mean? You think Mr. Goran burned down his own barn?" It wasn't possible. It just wasn't. "He would never do such a thing, Aunt Ginny. He couldn't."

"First of all, it really doesn't matter what I think, because it's not my case." She sounded angry about that. "Second, it has nothing to do with you. Your job right now is to get better. And third, who says he couldn't have set that fire himself?"

"Mr. Goran is afraid of fire."

Aunt Ginny snorted. "After what happened, he should be."

"No, Aunt Ginny, you don't understand. He's *really* afraid of fire. He wouldn't even let his wife have a gas stove."

"According to him, no doubt."

I told her what had happened when the barbecue tipped over. She wasn't impressed.

"Did it ever occur to you that Mr. Goran might have been using you to try to establish an alibi?"

That's the main trouble with cops—they're suspicious of everyone and everything.

"Do me a favor and stay out of it, Riley. I don't want to be looking for lost dogs for the rest of my career in this town."

"Lost dogs?"

"Well, technically, lost *dog*, singular. The mayor's wife's prizewinning shih tzu. It's missing, and the mayor's wife thinks it's been kidnapped. And since she's the mayor's wife..." She shook her head in disgust. "How did you and Stella get along?"

"Great. But seriously, Aunt Ginny, you don't really think Mr. Goran set his own barn on fire, do you?"

"If there's one thing I've learned on the job, Riley, it's that people aren't always what they seem."

"He told me he saved up for a long time to buy that farm. Why would he burn down the barn?"

"People generally commit arson for one of two reasons: insurance fraud or to cover up some other crime. In Mr. Goran's case, I'm guessing he needed the money."

"Couldn't he just have got a loan from the bank?"

"I don't know. It's not my case."

"And why would he set the barn on fire and then be *in* it while it was burning?"

"Fires can easily get out of control. Which is a very good reason not to commit arson." She sniffed the air. "Spaghetti sauce?"

"Lasagna. Stella made it."

"Are you hungry?"

I wasn't.

"You get some rest," Aunt Ginny said. "I'm starving."

Going up to my room was depressing. The one yellow wall, the abandoned cans of paint and the roller in the paint tray all reminded me that things might have turned out differently if I'd done what I was told to do. It took me forever to get to sleep, and once I did, Aunt Ginny shook me awake every few hours to make sure I was okay. I lay in the dark for a long time, thinking about Mr. Goran—nice, friendly Mr. Goran—trapped in his burning barn, reliving the nightmare that had plagued him for years.

THREE

One thing quickly became clear: having to rest all day, every day, was going to drive me crazy. I offered to help Stella. She politely but firmly refused the offer. I decided to finish painting my room to pass the time. She confiscated my roller and paint tray. I thought maybe I could ride my bike into town. It turned out I couldn't because Aunt Ginny had taken the precaution (her word, not mine) of slipping my bike-lock key off my key chain and sliding it onto hers. There was nothing to do but count the hours until my next doctor's appointment.

Four days after I was released from the hospital, Stella drove me back for my checkup. I passed every test with flying colors.

"So I can do everything I was doing before?" I asked the doctor.

"You can *start* doing *some* things. But no strenuous activity—no contact sports, no running, no gymnastics. You may find that you're more tired than usual and that you have trouble concentrating. If you get any of the symptoms on this information sheet"—he handed it to me—"tell someone immediately. Otherwise, I'll see you in a couple of weeks. Okay?"

It was more than okay! As soon as Aunt Ginny came home that night, I made her hand over my bike key. She insisted that Stella stay for another two days, but overall she was pleased with my progress.

"Have you heard anything about Mr. Goran?" I asked. "Is he going to be okay?"

"He hasn't regained consciousness. He may not make it, Riley. And if he does..." She looked grim. "As badly burned as he is, he'll be in for a lot of operations before he's back on his feet again—if he's ever back on his feet."

I was lying on the couch the next night, watching TV, when something hit the floor with a thud—Aunt Ginny's briefcase.

I had to crane my neck to see her in the front hall. "Tough day?"

Her jacket flew onto the arm of the nearest chair, hung for a moment and then slid to the floor.

Thunk. That was her gun in its holster. She was supposed to lock it up.

Jingle, jingle, clank. She dropped her car keys into a metal bowl on the small table near the foot of the stairs.

Another *thunk*, but sharper this time. Cell phone, hitting the surface of the table.

I sat up. Aunt Ginny's expression was a mixture of disgust and impatience.

"I'm guessing you didn't find the mayor's wife's dog," I said.

"She came home of her own accord." For some reason, Aunt Ginny did not seem pleased.

"So everyone is happy?" I ventured.

"Everybody except the mayor, the mayor's wife, the chief and my boss." She kicked off her shoes. They arced across the room one after another and landed, *thud, thud.*

"Shouldn't the mayor's wife be glad to have her dog back?"

"The mayor's wife took the dog in for a checkup. It's pregnant."

"The dog wasn't spayed?"

"The dog is a champion. The mayor's wife hoped she'd be the mother of champions. Not mutts."

"I thought it was usually the males—"

Aunt Ginny held up a hand. I took the hint and stopped talking.

"The mayor's wife gave the mayor grief, so he complained to the chief, who told my boss that a smart detective should have been able to find the dog because—and I quote—*a champion shih tzu is hardly a needle in a haystack.*"

"That dog could have been anywhere," I said. "And shih tzus are really small."

"You know that, and I know that, but apparently the rest of the world is insane. And then there are the guys."

"Guys?"

"My co-workers. They're like children. One left a whoopee cushion on my chair. Only ten-year-olds think whoopee cushions are funny. A couple of others have been making prank phone calls—at a police station!" She kicked her shoes from the middle of the floor, where they had landed, and flopped down into an armchair. "I thought when I got hired here that things would be different. Instead, I'm chasing dogs and surrounded by grown men acting like adolescents. I might as well have stayed where I was."

"It's been less than two weeks, Aunt Ginny. You have to be patient."

Aunt Ginny shot me a look of irritation. "What about the arson? Do you know how much I would have loved to work an arson investigation? Do you know how much I could have learned? But no. Mr. Whoopee Cushion got the case, along with Mr. Prank Phone Calls."

"I guess this isn't a good time to tell you that there's something wrong with the washing machine," I said. It wasn't. She scowled at me. The only surefire way to calm Aunt Ginny down was to give her something to eat. "There's some of Stella's meatloaf left over," I said.

"I can make potatoes and carrots. You have time for a shower."

Like a bone to a dog, it worked.

"I'll be down in ten minutes."

And she was, on the dot. She tucked into her supper with gusto and was smiling by the time she pushed her empty plate aside. "That was great. Thanks."

"Can I get you anything else?"

She shook her head and, with a sigh, rose from her chair to take her dishes to the sink. As she rinsed them, her face settled into a frown.

"Mr. Goran lives alone, right?" she said. "No wife, no kids, right?"

"He has a son."

"Does he live over there?"

"No. Is something wrong, Aunt Ginny?"

"Mr. Goran is in the hospital, but there's a light on in his house." She put down the plate she was rinsing and headed for the living room. I followed and found her on her hands and knees, looking for her shoes.

"It could be an intruder," she muttered. "It's been on the news that he's in the hospital. Maybe somebody decided to take advantage of that. I'm going to check it out. Aha!" She held up one shoe.

"I'll come with you."

"You'll do no such thing. This is police business."

She found her other shoe, jammed her foot into it and grabbed her car keys, her badge and her gun. I ran after her.

"It's faster to cut across the yard," I said. We had a long driveway. So did Mr. Goran, and his was on the side of his property farthest from us.

"I don't know what I'm going to find over there. I want to be prepared."

I jumped into the passenger seat before she could stop me.

"Riley, I said no!"

"If you don't hurry, the intruder will get away."

She scowled as she turned the key in the ignition. "You're staying in the car—or else." The car leaped forward, shooting gravel in all directions. She was about to turn onto the road when a car, its lights extinguished, shot past us from the direction of Mr. Goran's place.

"He's speeding," Aunt Ginny growled. "And his lights are either nonoperational or they're out on purpose. Either way—"

"Do you think he's the burglar?"

She cast another glance at the car—or, rather, at where the car had been. It was already out of sight. She slapped the steering wheel in disgust and made the turn for Mr. Goran's. Two minutes later she was out of the car and on her way to the porch. I rolled my window down so I could hear what was happening.

The front door was half open. Aunt Ginny approached with caution, her weapon drawn. She was about to step inside the house when a man appeared. His hands shot into the air when he came face-to-face with the gun, and Aunt Ginny said, "Police."

His voice carried clearly in the still summer night. "I'm Aram Goran. This is my father's house."

The son Mr. Goran was so worried about.

"Identification," Aunt Ginny demanded. She kept her weapon pointed at him.

He reached for a pocket.

"Slowly," Aunt Ginny cautioned.

Out came a wallet. He opened it and held it under the porch light for her to read. As soon as she lowered her gun, I jumped out of the car.

"I saw a light on in the house," Aunt Ginny said. "I thought maybe someone had broken in."

"Someone did break in," Aram Goran said. "There was a car in the driveway when the taxi dropped me off. At first I thought it must be my father's. There was a light on in the house, and the door was open. I went inside and called for my father. Someone ran out of his study. He practically tackled me on his way out the door. Then he took off in his car." He bent his elbow slowly. "I may need an X-ray."

"I think we passed him on our way here," Aunt Ginny said. "Did you get a good look at him?"

Aram shook his head. "He went by too fast, and the only light on was in the study. Did you get his license plate number?"

I answered for Aunt Ginny. "No. And his headlights were off."

Aram looked around Aunt Ginny at me. He was tall with dark piercing eyes and thick black hair, and he was wearing a suit complete with tie, despite the heat of the evening. He didn't look anything like his father.

"My niece," Aunt Ginny said curtly, sending a sharp look my way. "I'd like to see the damage, if you don't mind. Riley, get back in the car."

Aram led her inside. I crept in after them. I wanted to know what was happening. I felt terrible about Mr. Goran and what the police thought he had done. If I could just convince Aunt Ginny...

Aram led her to the study, which had clearly been ransacked. There were papers everywhere. All the desk drawers were open, their contents spilled onto the floor. Most of the books had been ripped from the shelves. A smashed laptop computer sat on the edge of the desk. Aunt Ginny was particularly interested in that.

"Whose computer is that? Your father's?"

"It's mine." Aram looked ruefully at it. "Rather, it *was* mine. It made an ominous sound when it hit the floor. It sounded even worse when I picked it up."

"Picked it up?"

"I was carrying it when the man attacked me."

"It wasn't in a case?" Aunt Ginny asked.

"I was using it in the taxi. Work never seems to stop." He sighed as he looked down at the broken computer. "It doesn't look good."

But Aunt Ginny was already scanning the place with her detective eyes. "Does your father keep anything of value in the house?"

Aram glanced around. "To be honest, I don't know. This is the first time I've been here."

"But you must know if your father owned any valuables—jewelry, art objects…"

"I'm afraid not. I haven't spoken to my father in a few years."

Aunt Ginny studied him for a moment.

"Well," she said finally, "there's definitely been a break-in. I'll take some pictures and dust for prints. That way, we might catch a break if there are any similar incidents reported in the area. But without knowing if anything was stolen, that's about all I can do for now." She excused herself to get her camera and fingerprint kit from the car.

While she was gone, I took a look around, beginning with the desk and ending with Aram's computer. He'd picked it up and was fiddling with it.

"It won't start," he said.

"Maybe it can be fixed."

He looked skeptical and shook the computer gently to make his point. It made a rattling sound that no computer should make. "As well, the screen is cracked. And it hit pretty hard. I was going to get a new one anyway."

"I have a friend who's a wizard with hard drives. If there's anything recoverable on yours, he might be able to retrieve it. Might be worth a try."

He still looked doubtful, but finally he said, "I don't think Steve Jobs himself would be able to retrieve anything off this thing. But be my guest." It took him a few minutes to wrestle the hard drive out of the computer. He handed it to me.

"Mr. Goran?" Aunt Ginny called. "May I speak with you for a moment?"

He left to find her. I slipped the hard drive into my pocket and went out onto the porch to wait.

A few minutes later, Aram came out and stood on the porch steps, where he stared up into the star-filled sky. That was one benefit of living in the country. The night came alive with stars and constellations that were invisible through all the ambient light—the streetlights and house lights and lights from office buildings—in the city.

"I'm sorry about your father," I said. "He's been nice to us."

"You know him?"

I told him how his father had welcomed us to our new house and planted a garden for us. He smiled when I said that.

"My father was—is—always planting things. Flowers, fruit trees, vegetables. He loves to see things grow."

"What about you? Did you inherit his green thumb?"

"I have no talent for growing. I'm nothing like my father."

"He told me he was worried about you."

He nodded. "I work for an aid agency in Afghanistan. My father doesn't approve."

"My dad is working near a rebel-held area in Liberia," I told him. "*I* don't approve."

He regarded me with new interest. Maybe he thought I would understand why he chose to work in a danger zone. But I didn't any more than I understood why my father chose to do the same thing, and why he kept volunteering to stay on.

"I wish I could have been here sooner, but it took a while to make the arrangements," he said. "The hospital here tracked me down. My father had me listed as his emergency contact, but the information was out of date. I spoke to his doctor. He says I may have to make some hard decisions."

"Did he tell you what happened?"

"When I stopped by the hospital, a policeman was there. He told me that my father had been in a barn fire." He peered through the darkness to where the barn had once stood, replaced now by a burnt-out skeleton and a heap of rubble. "He said the fire was set deliberately."

I admit I was curious, but I just couldn't make myself ask if the same police officer had mentioned that Mr. Goran was the prime suspect.

Aunt Ginny emerged from the house with her equipment.

"I'll file a report. I wish I could do more, Mr. Goran."

"Thank you," he said. "And please—it's Aram."

"It took him long enough to get here," Aunt Ginny muttered as we drove back down Mr. Goran's long driveway. "The fire was over a week ago."

"Mr. Goran's son works in Afghanistan," I pointed out. "Besides, he and his father were estranged."

"Is that what he told you?"

"His father told me."

"Did he also tell you what it was about?"

"He said Aram blames him for his mother's death."

"Oh?" That caught Aunt Ginny's interest. "Why? What happened?"

"She died of a heart attack. Mr. Goran told me his son thinks he worked his wife too hard. But he says she wanted to work. She wanted to save the money to buy a farm, and she never told him she had a heart condition. If he had known, things would have been different."

Aunt Ginny glanced at me.

"You're a good kid," she said—a first. "But you have to be careful with that."

"With what?"

"Believing whatever people tell you. You barely know the man, Riley. So just because he tells you something doesn't make it true, not until you know he's someone you can trust. And even then…"

And even then, you couldn't ever be sure that you really knew someone. That's what she meant.

Before I went to bed, I sent a text message to IT, who used to be one of Jimmy's roadies. The guys used to call him "It" because he was the Mount Everest of men and was reputed to have once carried an upright piano up two flights of stairs single-handedly, although I never met anyone who had actually seen him perform this astounding feat. IT preferred to think of himself as Mr. Information Technology, because he knew everything there was to know about computers and had taken care of all the web-based technology for Jimmy and the band. After Jimmy died, he'd started doing freelance tech support for several other bands. If Aram Goran's hard drive had anything retrievable on it, IT would be able to recover it.

He texted me back immediately and said he'd take a look at it. I promised to ship it to him the next day.

FOUR

After Aunt Ginny left for work the next morning, I painted another wall in my room. I wanted to keep going, because I was impatient to unpack and organize my things. But I had promised the doctor I would take it easy, so I took a break before tackling the third wall. I ate lunch, packaged up Aram Goran's hard drive and rode into town to post it.

Riding a bicycle on a country road is trickier than riding in the city. Sure, there's less traffic in the country, and that's good. But the cars and trucks that are on the road zoom by, unlike slower-moving city traffic, and the road I was on was a two-lane blacktop with a straight two-inch drop from the pavement to the gravel alongside it. That drop could throw a person off balance. I know that because when a truck raced past me close enough to graze my shoulder, I panicked, swerved and ended up slipping off the pavement. The gravel gripped my tires and almost stopped me dead. I just missed ending up in the deep ditch that ran between the gravel and the field on the other side. Also, it quickly became clear that people around here weren't used to sharing the road with cyclists. Two pickup-truck drivers and one other motorist yelled at me, "Get off the road, you dumb kid." I was relieved when I finally reached Moorebridge's town center.

Aunt Ginny and I had driven through town on our first day here. The place looked pretty small. My only other visits had been to the hardware store and the hospital on the outskirts of town. This trip confirmed my first impression. The mostly commercial main street was exactly twelve blocks long. The side streets had businesses for the first block and then quickly gave way to churches and houses. According to Aunt Ginny, more than two-thirds of the people in Moorebridge County lived in more rural areas, either on farms or in houses spaced out on the highway or on the roads leading to and from the other towns—villages, really—in the area.

But for a small place, there were a lot of people on the street, probably because it was summer and because Moorebridge was on a large lake with long sandy beaches that attracted tourists. Also, school was out, so there were lots of kids hanging around with seemingly nothing to do. I smiled as I passed them, but hardly anyone smiled back. Maybe they were surly locals. Or maybe they were bored city kids on vacation.

I spotted a supermarket on the main road just west of town and made a note to go back there later to buy some fruit and veggies. But first I went to the post office, which was a small counter at the rear of the pharmacy. The clerk said it would take three days at the most to get the package to IT. I sauntered down the main street and bought a local newspaper, which I took to a coffee shop—the Sip 'n' Bite.

The place was packed with people enjoying snacks or beverages and some conversation. I found a vacant table and sat down, then leafed through the paper for news about the arson case. There was nothing.

A waitress came over. "What'll it be, honey?"

"Iced tea, please."

She frowned as she peered down at me. "Hey, you're that girl, aren't you?"

"What girl?"

"The one whose picture was in the paper last week. The girl who called the fire department."

"My picture was in the paper?"

"Sure." She tucked her order pad into her apron pocket and strode across the café to a bulletin board beside the cash register. From where I was sitting, I could see that it had a section for items for sale and another for upcoming events. News articles were tacked in one corner. The waitress removed one and brought it back to me.

"See?" She held it out. Sure enough, there was a picture of me from last year, when I'd figured out where the money from an old robbery was hidden. "It says you got hurt trying to rescue that Goran fella."

"He's our next-door neighbor."

"Well, he's lucky it's you who lives beside him and not a lot of other folks around here."

"What do you mean?"

"Sharon, order up!" someone barked. My waitress—Sharon, apparently—shouted that she was coming.

"I'll be back in a jiffy with your tea," she said, flashing me a smile.

I read the article while I waited. It was from the local paper, and it didn't tell me anything I didn't already know. Sharon brought my iced tea, took the article from me and reposted it on the bulletin board. I sat back and sipped my tea. I couldn't help over-hearing the people around me.

"If he lives, he'll clear out for sure." That came from a middle-aged woman at the next table. Was she talking about Mr. Goran?

"If he lives, that will just get Ted more riled up," said her companion, another middle-aged woman.

The first woman caught me listening and fixed me with a stern look. "Can I help you with something?" Her tone made it clear that helping me was the last thing she intended to do.

I shook my head and turned back to my news-paper, my cheeks burning. The two women lowered their voices. I finished my iced tea quickly and took my bill to the cash register. While I waited for Sharon to appear, I glanced at the bulletin board. All the news-paper articles that had been tacked up had to do with Mr. Goran. The oldest one, yellowed and curling at the corners, was headed *Foreign owner buys Winters farm at auction.* Another much smaller one was from the weekly crime roundup: *Vandalism at local farm.* Someone had scrawled under it, *Not enough.* Not enough what? Not enough vandalism? There were several articles about the fire besides the one with my picture.

"Looks like the fire was big news," I said when Sharon came out of the kitchen, wiping her hands on her apron.

"Let's just say people have an interest." She took my money. "Don't let anyone give you a hard time for what you did. It's not your fault you live next door."

I wanted to ask her what she meant, but another cry of "Order's up" sent her scurrying away.

I spotted a florist shop—Carol's Flowers for All Occasions—on a side street, and I went inside.

"Can I help you?" A woman in a green apron appeared from the back room in response to a jingling bell above the door. The rose-shaped pin on her apron bib identified her as Carol.

"I want some flowers, but I'm not sure what to get."

"What's the occasion?"

"It's for someone in the hospital."

"Happy occasion? Hopeful occasion? Sad occasion?"

Happy occasion? In a *hospital*?

"Did she just have a baby?" Carol asked, reading my mind. "Or is it someone recovering from an operation? Or someone who got bad news?"

I wasn't even sure Mr. Goran was going to know the flowers were there, but I decided to stay hopeful, because I hoped he was going to be okay. Carol showed me a selection of bright, long-lasting flowers. After I made my selection, she asked if I wanted them delivered or if I preferred to take them myself.

"I'll take them myself." While she wrapped the flowers, I asked if she knew Mr. Goran.

"The man who burned down his own barn?" She shook her head. "He never came in here. Are the flowers for him?"

"He's my next-door neighbor."

"Ah," she said, nodding as if I had just answered an important question. "I thought I recognized you. You're the girl from the paper. Well, he's lucky to have you for a neighbor."

That was the second time I had heard that today. "What do you mean?"

She shook her head as if she was sorry she had spoken.

"My aunt and I are new in town," I told her. "Is there something wrong with Mr. Goran?"

"Well…" She glanced around, even though we were alone. "As I said, I don't know him. But I guess you could say he hasn't made himself popular. I've lived here for ten years, and by and large the people are nice. But there are plenty of them who, if they'd been in your shoes that night, might not have made that call."

She had to be kidding. "Why not?"

The bell above the door jingled. Two women came in. Carol handed me my flowers and said she hoped my friend would get better soon.

I put the flowers in my bike's carrier basket and rode to the hospital, where a nurse told me that Mr. Goran wasn't allowed any visitors.

"Can you make sure he gets these?" I asked, holding out my bouquet.

The nurse took them and smelled them. "They're pretty," she said. "They'll look lovely beside the plant he received."

"Someone else sent something?" I was glad to hear that. It meant that not everyone felt the way Carol had been hinting they did.

"Not sent. Dropped off," the nurse said. "Too bad she didn't include a card so I could tell him who they're from."

"So he's awake now?"

"I'm afraid not. His son is in with him now."

I was glad to hear that too. I left my name so that when the time came, the nurse could tell Mr. Goran I'd been there.

Before heading home, I stopped by the supermarket I'd spotted on my way into town. The cashier at the checkout was a flaming redhead (dyed, I think), about my age. Her name tag read *Ashleigh*.

"You live here in town?" I asked.

"Yeah." She punched in a code for a container of strawberries. "What about you? Tourist?"

"New kid in town."

She glanced up from her scanner. "Where from?"

I told her.

"Poor you," she said. "For being dragged here, I mean. I can't wait to graduate high school so I can leave."

"It can't be that bad."

She snorted. "Spoken like someone who wasn't born here in Tinytown." She punched in codes for cantaloupe, grapes and apples. "I guess you'll be going to Lyle, huh?"

"Lyle?"

"L.S. Murcheson Comprehensive. The high school. The *L* stands for Lyle. He was, like, the first mayor here or something."

She rang up my tomatoes, cucumber, peppers and lettuce and told me the grand total. I dug out the grocery money Aunt Ginny had left me.

"You know, if you want good local veggies, you should try the market on Wednesdays and Saturdays at the beach."

"Market?"

"It's a combination flea market and farmers' market. Everything there is picked the same day, and it tastes a lot better than the imported stuff this place stocks. But don't tell anyone I said so." She grinned at me.

"Thanks for the tip."

"What's your name?"

"Riley."

"Riley." I guess she approved, because she smiled. "There's a beach party every Saturday night. The kids around here all go. You interested? I mean, you're going to have to meet the local dweebs sooner or later. You might as well get the lay of the land before school starts. You can come with me. I get off at nine on Saturday."

"Okay. Sure." Why not?

"Meet me here." She grinned and started to ring in another order.

FIVE

The doorbell rang while I was making a salad to go with supper. It was Aram, holding a basket filled with vegetables.

"These are from my father's farm," he said. "To thank you."

"Thank me? What for?"

"For the flowers. And for calling the fire department the night of the fire."

Someone must have told him.

"While I was waiting to see my father, I picked up an old newspaper. You were in it."

Oh.

"If it hadn't been for you, he might have died in that barn."

"I just did what anyone would have done in my place."

He gave me an odd look but didn't say anything more about the fire. Instead he said, "Where would you like me to put this?"

"I can take it."

He shook his head. "It's heavy."

"Okay. You can put it in the kitchen." I led the way.

He set the basket down on the kitchen counter. "There is so much produce ripening in the fields and gardens. I don't know what to do with it. At least this lot won't go to waste."

"What was your father going to do with it?"

"I've been looking at what records I can find. As far as I can see, he trucks most of it into the city. There are farmers' markets in different locations every day of the week. But I don't want to be away every day. I want to be here until I know if he will recover. Still, I hate the idea of things going to waste. Maybe I've spent too much time in third-world countries."

"Why don't you sell some of it at the market in Moorebridge?" I told him what Ashleigh had told me. "If you want, I can see about getting a table."

Aram hesitated. "I don't know anything about selling vegetables. I wouldn't even know how much to charge."

"I can find out for you. And I can see about getting a stall. I can do the selling too." It wasn't as if I had a million other things on my agenda.

"I couldn't ask you to do so much. You're still recovering from that night yourself."

"You don't have to ask me. I'm volunteering. I want to help. I like your father."

He flashed a smile that changed his whole face from sour to sweet.

"Okay."

I rode back into town the next day to make arrangements for the market, but I wasn't sure where to start, so I dropped by the local newspaper office. Someone there would know for sure. The woman behind the counter—she turned out to be the publisher—was a great source of information. She told me where to go to reserve a stall (the municipal building), how much it cost (nothing), and even how much business the typical stall did (*If it's a sunny day and your produce is good, you'll probably sell out by closing, which is two o'clock*). From there, it was easy. I went to the municipal building to apply for and receive a stall number and a license to have with me on market day in case an inspector showed up. I went back to the grocery store to check out how much their produce was so that I had something to go by when pricing Mr. Goran's vegetables. I went to a dollar store and bought price stickers, paper bags and some markers. Then I headed home. Well, actually, I headed for Mr. Goran's farm.

Aram wasn't there, but there was a late-model car parked near one of the farm buildings. I hadn't seen it from the road. Nor had I seen the two men who were wandering around the property. One was tall and muscular, in jeans, a T-shirt and a denim jacket. The other was shorter and thinner and wearing a business suit. He was the one who spotted me first.

"Hello, young lady. How are you this fine day?" His smile was as bright as a new penny.

"Mr. Goran isn't home."

"Yes I see that no one appears to be here at the moment. I saw all the damage…" He nodded at what used to be the barn. "I was wondering if maybe the owner—Mr. Goran—might be in the market to sell."

"He's in the hospital."

"I did hear that. Unfortunate."

"His son is in town."

The man in the suit cocked his head to one side and studied me. "You seem to be pretty up-to-date on the Gorans' affairs. By gosh, but you look familiar. We haven't met, by any chance? Are you one of the Goran clan?"

"I live next door."

He grinned. "That's it! I knew it." He snapped his fingers. "You're that girl from the newspaper, the one who called the fire department. Riley, is it?" He looked as pleased as if he had pulled a rabbit out of a hat.

I nodded.

"Well, Riley, you're quite the local hero. As I say, I was just looking around. I heard the owner had been badly hurt in the fire. I imagine he won't be farming again, and I'm interested in taking the place off his hands." He pulled something out of his pocket. "My card."

"I'll give it to Aram."

"Aram?"

"Mr. Goran's son."

He handed me his card. Donald Curtis, realtor. No company name.

"Well then." He flashed another toothy smile. "I'll be on my way." He nodded to his companion, whom he had not introduced. They climbed into the car. The big man drove.

After they were gone, I left a note for Aram, asking him to call me so we could make plans for the market. I pushed it and Mr. Curtis's business card through the letter slot. Then I did what Mr. Curtis had done—I took a good look around.

Everything on the farm was well kept, from the stone house surrounded by flower gardens and shrubs to the equipment shed, the garage with the tractor and the pickup truck in it, and the workshop (locked) with its workbench and array of tools. The barn, of course, was a tangled mess of blackened wood and wet ash. But before the fire it had been as neat and well maintained as any barn could be—except for a small hole in one wall that Mr. Goran was going to patch to keep out small animals. I'd seen the inside of the barn.

Mr. Goran had been proud to give me a tour. Now two walls were badly charred but still standing, although signs had been posted warning of danger.

But apart from the devastated barn, the farm was picture-perfect. Mr. Goran had worked his whole life to scrape together the money to buy the place. Why would he destroy it—especially in the way it had been done? He was terrified of fire. I'd seen that for myself. He'd even refused to allow his wife to have the gas stove she coveted. Even if he had needed the money, which was what Aunt Ginny had hinted, would he have gone about it that way, through arson? I couldn't imagine it. Not in a million years.

SIX

Aunt Ginny came in after midnight. I knew because she flung her shoes across the front hall, hitting the table near the stairs and knocking over the little lamp on top of it. It crashed to the floor, jolting me awake. I thought someone had broken into the house, and, heart pounding, I crept to the top of the stairs with my baseball bat.

"What on earth do you think you're doing?" Aunt Ginny demanded when she saw me.

"I thought someone smashed a window and was breaking in."

"And you were planning to do what, exactly? Didn't I teach you better than that?"

I deduced that she was in a foul mood. "What if I'd called 9-1-1 instead?" I asked. "And what if one of your new colleagues rushed out here only to find out that *you* were the cause of the call?"

She muttered something unintelligible.

"Bad day, Aunt Ginny?"

"I didn't sign on to be a pet detective."

"Another lost dog?"

"Not lost. Abused."

"Isn't that a job for animal welfare?"

"Yes. And they investigated. Then they called us, and, of course, I got the case. The dog, which doesn't have any tags, was badly beaten. I'm supposed to find out who did it."

"Badly beaten? Is it okay?"

"It's going to be a long recovery."

"Poor thing. Who would do something like that?"

"You sound just like the chief. I like dogs as much as the next person." When I gave her a skeptical look, she said, "Just because I don't choose to live with one doesn't mean I don't respect them as fellow citizens of this world." That sounded rehearsed to me. "But I don't want to end up as a pet detective. That's not what I worked for so hard all these years. I need a shower."

"Aunt Ginny, about the washing machine—." The laundry situation was getting desperate.

"I said I'd handle it, and I will," said Aunt Ginny. "But right now I'm going to bed."

Aunt Ginny was snoring the next morning when I peeked into her room. Then I crept downstairs. I left her a note and went outside to wait for Aram.

He arrived exactly at seven in his father's pickup, its bed filled with baskets of vegetables. We drove to the market down by the beach and unloaded at our stall, and I taped a sign to it: *Goran Farm*. Then I started writing out price signs.

"How's your father?" I asked as I set out brilliant-green cucumbers, ears of freshly picked corn, green beans, field tomatoes, peppers and onions.

"There's been no change. I get the impression the doctors aren't expecting much."

"There were two men at the farm yesterday. One of them said he was interested in buying the place."

"Mr. Curtis?"

I nodded.

"I got his card. But it's my father's farm. Any decision regarding it is up to him."

I didn't want to think how upset Mr. Goran would be if he was forced to sell his beloved farm.

The stalls around us began to fill up. I couldn't help noticing that people were staring at us. Some of them whispered to one another. The ones who stared the longest and hardest were at the Winters Farm stall. I glanced at Aram. He was staring right back at them.

"Do you know those people?" I asked.

"I know the farm my father bought belonged to a man named Winters."

The man who was staring came out of his stall. The woman with him—his wife?—grabbed his arm and tried to pull him back, but he shook her off. He marched toward us.

"Who are you?" he demanded of Aram.

"Aram Goran. My father owns Goran Farm."

The man's face twisted in disgust, as if he'd bitten into something rancid.

"And you are…?" Aram said.

"Ted Winters. Your father stole my father's farm."

Aram stayed perfectly calm despite Mr. Winters's belligerence. "As I understand it, my father bought his farm at auction."

"He had no business being at that auction."

"Ted!" The same woman who had tried to hold Mr. Winters back ran over and grabbed his arm. "Ted, we have to get ready."

Ted Winters glowered at Aram for another moment before letting his wife lead him away. But once he was back at his own stall, he kept staring at Aram.

"What is he talking about, stealing?" Aram asked. "Why would he say that?"

I had no idea. But I bet it tied in with what Sharon the waitress and Carol the florist had said—that there were people who wouldn't have called the fire department that night.

"I can finish getting ready while you visit your father," I said. "I'll be fine." It might be good for him to get away. Mr. Winters's staring was making me nervous.

Aram agreed. "I would like to tell Father what we're doing. The doctor says I should talk to him. He says it might help." He looked at the produce piled high on the table. "Are you sure you'll be all right?"

"Positive. I have everything I need. But when you come back, can you bring some more change? Just in case."

He left, and I finished setting up. People were already sauntering among the stalls. It wasn't long before I was bagging beans and cucumbers, tomatoes and corn. Most of the stalls seemed to be busy, but I heard a few people say that my prices were better than those at other stalls. I had a steady flow of customers.

It was a hot day, and all the talking I was doing was making me thirsty. I wished Aram would return so I could get a cold drink. Some kids wandered over. There were a dozen of them, maybe more, all boys. I didn't pay close attention to the whole group because one of them, a tall boy with a mop of dirty-blond hair, stepped up close and demanded to know who I was.

I told him my name and waited for him to tell me his.

He didn't.

He ran his hand over ears of corn, cucumbers, tomatoes.

"Nice," he said. He glanced at his buddies. A couple of them had pressed close to the table. The rest stood back half a pace. A girl stood behind them. Her eyes were on the blond boy. She was watching as if she wanted to talk to him, and she looked nervous. She was shifting from foot to foot and turning what looked like a large coin over and over in one hand, like a magician practicing a coin trick.

"Can I help you?" I asked the boy.

"Yeah, you can. Can you step back a little?"

"What?"

Before I could do anything to stop them, the boys closest to the table flipped it over. Tomatoes, corn, carrots, beets cascaded to the ground.

"Oops, sorry," the blond boy said. He didn't sound remotely apologetic. If anything, he seemed pleased with himself. "Let us give you a hand."

But instead of picking things up, as I was doing, he and his friends started to stomp all over the vegetables on the ground.

"Hey!" I was furious. I grabbed the boy by the arm. "If you don't stop that, I'll—" I had been going to say that I was going to call the cops—well, Aunt Ginny—and I started to dig my cell phone out of my pocket. But someone grabbed it from me—I didn't see who—and someone else shoved me aside. Again,

I didn't see who. I glanced around, but the boys who were standing farther away from the table had formed a kind of screen, blocking my stall from view and stopping everyone except the girl from seeing what they were doing, and she was only able to see because she had moved in closer.

I started to elbow through the boys to get help. Someone grabbed me from behind and held me back. I kicked him. He yowled but didn't let go. I struggled as basket after basket of produce was reduced to pulp before my eyes. Someone else shouted.

"Hey, what's going on there?"

The boys drifted away, keeping their backs to the rows of stall. A man rushed up to me and asked if I was okay. He offered to call the police, but I said I would handle it. Ted Winters, across the way, stared wide-eyed at the destruction. He turned to search out the boys, who by then had disappeared from view. He started to come out of his own stall but then abruptly stopped.

"What happened?" said someone behind me. It was Aram. He was carrying a frosty bottle of lemonade. He handed it to me as he took in the devastation. "Who did this?"

"Some kids." I located my cell phone in a puddle of smashed tomatoes and wiped it off with a paper bag. "I'm calling the police."

Aram looked at the curious faces of shoppers and the hard faces of the neighboring stallholders. I think we both saw the uniformed police officer at the same time. He stopped at Mr. Winters's booth. Mr. Winters pointed to ours. The cop frowned, took in the scene and came across to us.

"What happened here?" he asked.

I glanced at Aram, who nodded at me and said, "Tell him what you just told me."

I repeated what I'd already said. "Some kids trashed our stall."

The cop bent down and picked up the sign that lay on the ground. "Goran, huh? Not the same Goran that set fire to his barn."

"My father's barn burned down, if that's what you mean," Aram said stiffly.

"And now some kids are giving you a hard time. Don't suppose you know their names?"

"I wasn't here when it happened."

"So no description of these kids either?" Maybe I was imagining things, but he didn't seem as interested as I knew Aunt Ginny would have been under the same circumstances.

"*I* was here," I said. "And I would *definitely* recognize the ringleader if I saw him again."

The cop gave me a slow once-over. "Are you a Goran too?"

"No. I'm a Donovan. You probably know my aunt, Virginia McFee."

The cop's eyes narrowed. "McFee?"

"She's a detective." I held up my cell phone. "Maybe I should call her."

"You may not be able to reach her. The animal crime around here is keeping her pretty busy." His lips twitched as he tried to keep from laughing. That made me angry.

"Then maybe I should go to the police station myself and file a complaint," I said. "Maybe I'll get lucky and find a police officer who at least tries to do his job."

The cop's face turned red. He reached into his pocket and pulled out a notebook. "Why don't you tell me all about this alleged attack on your vegetables?"

I told him everything I could—the number of kids who had surrounded the table, a description of the tall kid, what he'd said, what they'd all done.

"Any witnesses?"

"They surrounded the table so that no one could see what they were doing. But you could ask around." Then I remembered. "There was a girl. She saw everything."

"What girl?"

"I don't know her name."

"Is there anything else you can tell me?"

"No."

He flipped his notebook shut. "Thank you for your cooperation." He turned to go.

"Wait a minute," I said. "You're not leaving, are you?"

"I'm going to see if I can scare up any witnesses. Then I'm going to write up a report and keep an eye out for the kid you described."

"What if I see him again?"

"Call us." He seemed impatient to go.

"Wait," I said again. He shot me a look of undiluted annoyance. "Aren't you going to give me your card?"

"I'm all out."

"Your name then?"

He looked me in the eye. "Shears. Brian Shears."

He walked across to the Winters's stall and spoke to Ted Winters, who shook his head. He approached another stall, and then another. All he got in return was more head-shaking. Meanwhile, Aram and I cleaned up the mess and packed our things. By then everyone else was winding down too. Aram offered me a ride home, but I decided to stay behind.

I was angry. Officer Shears couldn't have been less helpful if he'd tried. I didn't know what his problem was, but there was no way I was going to let the incident slide. I went from stall to stall and talked to the people who were packing up for the day. Some people seemed sincere when they told me they'd been surprised to glance over and see everything on the ground. Some were too far away to have noticed the commotion. But there were other people, people whose booths were close by, who seemed less than genuine when they said they'd seen nothing amiss. Some of them didn't look me in the eye when they spoke to me. None of them had any idea who the tall boy was that I described to them, even though most of them had signs that advertised their farms as being in Moorebridge. Were they some of the people who wouldn't have lifted a finger to call the fire department? What did they have against Mr. Goran?

SEVEN

I walked up and down every street and alley in town, but I didn't see the tall boy or any of his friends. Or the girl who had silently watched the whole thing.

When I finally gave up, exhausted, I realized that I would have to walk home—unless I asked Aunt Ginny for a ride. After the mood she'd been in the night before, I decided to take the exercise option.

By the time I reached our driveway, I was sticky and sweaty. I let myself into the house, had a shower, got something to eat and stretched out on a chaise under a massive oak tree behind the house. I didn't budge until Aunt Ginny shook me awake.

"I've been calling you," she said. "I even tried your cell."

"It's in the house. What time is it?"

"After six. I bought chicken. Let's get supper ready."

When Aunt Ginny buys chicken, she doesn't mean chicken that you can roast or fry. She means a ready-to-eat chicken. If I'm lucky, it's barbecued chicken from a grocery store. If I'm unlucky, it's fried chicken pieces from a fast-food joint. This time it was a barbecued chicken. We made a salad to go with it and ate on the patio.

"Did you find the dog beater?" I asked.

"As a matter of fact, I did. One good thing about a small town: there's always someone who notices something." That sure hadn't been my experience, not today anyway. "I kept asking around until I found a woman who'd heard about someone who supposedly said something to someone else about hearing a dog yelping as if it was being beaten. I tracked down that person, and she pointed me to a man who heard his neighbor's dog yowling a few nights ago. I showed him a picture, so I knew it was his neighbor's dog. When I talked to the neighbor, he said his dog had run off. He also said he knew nothing about any beating and that someone else must have hurt the dog after it ran away. But I finally got him to confess."

"How?"

Aunt Ginny grinned. "I told him what a pain dogs are and how much I hated having to chase them down to satisfy people like the mayor's wife who put animal welfare above people welfare. Then I told him about a dog I had once that never shut up and how I'd got a friend of mine to drive it far away and dump it so I could tell my parents he'd run away." I must have looked horrified, because she added, "Relax, Riley. I was spinning him a story. And it worked. He told me what a pain his dog was and that it needed a few smacks from time to time to learn who was boss. I arrested him."

"But you lied to him!"

"Standard operating procedure—deceit in the name of justice. Cops do it all the time."

"But you're the good guys. At least, some of you are."

"Sometimes the good guys have to trick the bad guys in order to catch them." She paused and frowned. "What do you mean by *some of you*?"

I told her what had happened at the market.

"You didn't tell me you were helping Aram. The note just said you were going into town."

"And I did—to help. But those kids ruined everything, and that cop didn't take it seriously."

"Did you get his name?"

"Shears."

She looked surprised. "I know him. He seems okay."

"People aren't always what they seem. Isn't that what you told me, Aunt Ginny?"

"I didn't mean cops. But I'll talk to him the next time I see him. I promise." She stood up to clear the table. "So, what do you want to do tonight? Are you up for a movie?"

"Actually, Aunt Ginny..." I told her about the party Ashleigh had invited me to.

"I don't know if that's a good idea, Riley. I don't know any of these kids. And after that concussion—"

"The doctor says I'm fine. And how am I going to meet any kids if I don't get out there? I don't want to show up at school as a complete stranger."

"But you don't know what goes on at these parties. Or how old some of the kids might be. Or what they might get into. There's no way I'm going to let you ride home with someone who's been drinking or indulging in anything that could cloud his or her judgment. You're *my* responsibility."

"Come on, Aunt Ginny. You know I'd never do anything that would get me into trouble."

She arched an eyebrow.

"It's just a bunch of kids getting together. If you drive me into town, you can meet Ashleigh, the girl who invited me. And I promise I'll call you when the party is over so you can come and get me. Please, Aunt Ginny?"

"I don't know…"

"I won't do anything stupid. I promise."

She thought it over for an agonizingly long time before she finally said, "Before I make a final decision, I get to ask Ashleigh a few questions. Deal?"

As if I had a choice.

We got to the supermarket just before nine. Ashleigh was closing out her cash drawer. She smiled when she saw me.

"I'm glad you came," she said.

I hoped she would feel the same way after she met my aunt.

"You must be Ashleigh," Aunt Ginny said before I could speak. "I'm Detective McFee."

I could have strangled her. Why couldn't she be just my aunt for once?

"Detective?" Ashleigh cast a troubled glance at me.

"My aunt is a cop." I hoped the tone of my voice conveyed that I was sorry I hadn't mentioned this fact earlier.

"I am indeed. What's your full name, Ashleigh?" She asked the question in her slightly intimidating on-duty cop voice.

"Um…" Ashleigh glanced at me again. She was probably sorry she had ever met me. "Wainwright, Ashleigh Marie Wainwright."

"The pharmacist down the street is named Wainwright," Aunt Ginny said.

"That's my dad. And my mom. They're both pharmacists."

Aunt Ginny nodded her approval. "Do they know you're planning to go to a beach party?"

"Yes."

"So if I were to ask them, they wouldn't be surprised?"

"No." Ashleigh looked perfectly calm now. "I go to beach parties all the time."

"How long have you been working here?"

"Since school ended in June. I'm hoping to stay on part-time after the summer. My parents think jobs teach kids the value of money and how to handle it properly."

Aunt Ginny liked that answer too. "Very sensible. All right then. I'll pick you up at eleven o'clock, Riley."

"Eleven? Things will just be getting started," Ashleigh said. "I don't have to be home until one."

Up went Aunt Ginny's left eyebrow. "That seems late for someone your age."

"We live right near the beach. My parents can practically see what we're doing from their bedroom window. Please don't make Riley leave so early. If you're worried, she can stay over at my place afterward." She looked at me. "You want to?"

"Sure. And I'll call you as soon as we get back there," I promised Aunt Ginny.

She thought this over. "I suppose I can always call Ashleigh's parents." She made it sound like a threat.

"The pharmacy is probably closing right now, which means they should be home by ten." Ashleigh grabbed a piece of cash-register tape and scrawled on it. "Here's our phone number."

Aunt Ginny stared at the slip of paper and then at me. "I *will* make that call," she said.

"So it's all okay? Riley can stay over?" Ashleigh smiled at me. "Great. Thanks."

Aunt Ginny gave a curt nod. "But I'll expect to hear from you the minute you're back at Ashleigh's," she said to me. "And make that call from her home phone, not your cell phone, understand?"

I said yes. She told me to keep my wits about me and left.

"Wow," Ashleigh said as she watched her go. "A cop for an aunt. That's like having a prison guard in the family, isn't it?"

"Yeah. Kind of."

"What's with the calling from my home phone? Have you used up all your minutes on your cell-phone plan?"

If only. "It's so she can know exactly where I am, which is impossible with a cell phone. If I call from your home phone, she'll know I'm at your house."

"Ouch," Ashleigh said. "Promise me you won't say anything about that to my parents when you meet them, okay?"

I wanted to make friends, not lose them. I promised.

The beach was deserted except for a few couples walking hand in hand in the last moments of sunset.

"Where is everybody?" I asked.

Ashleigh laughed. "You don't have a beach party where everyone—especially adults—can see it."

"But you told my aunt—"

"—that you could see the party from my house? You can—if you go up on the roof with a pair of binoculars. Don't worry. There's never any trouble. Nothing bad is going to happen."

As we walked along the beach, the houses on the shore got farther and farther apart. After we rounded a point, there was just shore and beach and woods.

"The conservation area starts just there." Ashleigh pointed to a sign up ahead. "There are no houses or cottages on this side of the point."

But there was a blazing fire out on the sand, where, accompanied by the beat of music, dozens of kids had gathered. Some were sitting in the glow of the flames, some were standing, a few were dancing. When we got closer, Ashleigh shouted a greeting. Two girls detached themselves from the group and came to meet her. Ashleigh introduced me to her "friends since we were kids"—Taylor Martin, pale and wispy with long blond hair, and Madison Smith.

Madison was raven-haired and slender. She was also the girl at the market who had seen my stall getting trashed.

"I've been looking for you," I said.

"Really?" Her tone was as icy as a January morning.

Ashleigh and Taylor stared at me. They were probably wondering the same thing—how could I have been looking for someone whom, as far as they knew, I had just met?

"I need a witness," I said.

"Witness to what?" Ashleigh asked.

"I have no idea what you're talking about," Madison said. She looked me right in the eye when she said it. For a second I was confused. Was I mistaken about who she was?

"At the market. You saw those boys who trashed my stall. Do you know any of them?"

Ashleigh shifted her gaze to Madison.

Madison shook her head. "I don't know what you mean." Before I could jog her memory, she turned and walked away.

"What was that about? What stall? Who trashed it?" Ashleigh asked.

"It's a long story." I didn't want to ruin the party mood, especially when I was the new kid in town.

Taylor gave me a sympathetic look. "Don't let Maddy get to you. She's in a bad mood. She has guy trouble."

"As in the guy she's hot for totally ignores her," Ashleigh said. She leaned closer to me. "You're going to tell me later all about what happened at that stall, and I mean it."

I promised I would.

We strolled closer to the fire, where the action was, and Ashleigh introduced me to more kids—so many that I doubted I would remember everyone's name. She announced that my aunt and I were new in town but said nothing about Aunt Ginny's job. I was grateful. I knew they would all find out sooner or later, but there was no reason it had to be right now. Taylor asked me a lot of questions. She wanted to know where I'd lived before and how come I was living with my aunt now. She was fascinated when I told her that I had more or less grown up on a tour bus with the famous sixties rocker Jimmy Donovan.

"My parents have a bunch of his CDs," she said. "They're not bad. It's only music my parents play that doesn't make me want to puke."

I wasn't surprised. Jimmy had survived on tour as long as he did because his music appealed to everyone. In fact, his fan base seemed to expand the older he got.

The kids I met all talked about people I didn't know or events I had never heard of, but I was used to that. I'd spent most of my life traveling with Jimmy and the band. That meant I was the new kid practically everywhere I went. Once school started, I would catch up.

After a while someone opened a cooler full of hot dogs, and someone else passed around sticks to roast them on. Bags of potato chips appeared. So did icy cans of soda. The music got louder, and more kids started dancing. From the way some of them were acting, I guessed they were drinking something other than soda. But Ashleigh wasn't into that. Neither were her friends. A boy named Charlie Edison asked me if I wanted to dance. He looked about my age and was my height, and he had a sweet, goofy smile. Ashleigh assured me he was okay, so I said yes. That's when the trouble started.

Charlie and I were dancing when someone stepped between us. A tall someone with a mop of dirty-blond hair. The ringleader from the market. He stood close to me—too close.

"Who invited *you*?" he demanded.

"What's your problem, Mike?" Charlie said.

Mike didn't even turn around to look at him. "No one's talking to you, Lightbulb." I later found out that "Lightbulb" was what some kids called Charlie because of his last name. Mike's eyes drilled into mine. "No one wants you here."

"Wrong as usual." Charlie circled Mike, who was at least a head and a half taller and much more muscular, and looked up at him. He didn't seem intimidated.

Mike shoved Charlie—so hard that Charlie ended up on his butt in the sand. The kids closest to the action stopped what they were doing and turned to watch.

"No one wants you here," Mike said again. He was so close that I could smell the hotdog on his breath.

Charlie jumped to his feet and tapped Mike on the shoulder.

"Hey, Beanstalk, for your information, I've been spending my summer studying. You want to see what I've learned so far?"

"Buzz off, Shortstop." Mike still didn't look at Charlie. He reserved his squinty little eyes for me and me alone. "If you were smart, you'd stay away from that Paki—and from me."

"Paki?" I hated that word. "I have no idea who you're talking about."

"He means the guy whose barn burned down," Charlie said.

I stared at Mike. "Then you're an idiot. Mr. Goran is from Turkey, not Pakistan."

"Whatever," Mike said. "And by the way, this is *my* beach and *my* beach party. You're not welcome here."

Right. Like he thought I was going to fall for that.

"It's not your beach. It's a public place, just like that conservation area." I nodded toward the shore.

Charlie tapped Mike on the shoulder again. "Ahem."

Mike spun around. "I told you to buzz off."

I'm not one hundred percent sure what happened next because it happened so fast. But for sure Charlie executed some kind of martial-arts move, and for sure Mike flew into the air and described a perfect arc before landing flat on his back in the sand. A collective *oooh!* went up from the crowd.

Charlie smiled down at Mike. "How about that?"

"Nice move," I said.

"When there are guys like Mike in this world, and when there are people like me who are, well, vertically challenged..." He shrugged. "I spent the first year of high school being shoved into lockers. I got sick of it. So I've been taking measures."

"And studying hard, I see." I didn't really approve of fighting, but it was quite a move.

Mike rolled over. Some kids hurried over to him. One of them, I noticed, was Madison.

"Are you okay, Mike?" she asked.

A couple of guys helped Mike to his feet. He was seething. He glared at Charlie—and at me.

"What's going on here?" someone—a man—demanded. I didn't remember seeing him around the fire.

"That's Ed," Charlie told me. "He's a park ranger—and a good guy."

Ed must have overheard him, because he said, "That's right, Charlie. I'm a good guy." If we'd been standing in daylight instead of the glow of a beach fire, I'm sure I would have seen Charlie's cheeks redden. "As long as there's no trouble on my turf, that is. No trouble means no fighting." He looked pointedly at Mike and his friends, who were lined up in menacing formation. "So again, what's going on?"

"She works for Goran," Mike said, jabbing a thumb at me. Some of the kids who weren't part of his posse peered at me with new interest. Some of their faces betrayed disdain. I was glad Ashleigh wasn't among that group. Neither was Charlie.

"I don't care if she works for the Wicked Witch of the West," Ed said. "No fighting, period. If I catch you guys at it again, I'll shut down your beach parties—for good. You got that?" He stared at Mike until Mike nodded. Then he turned and looked at every face in turn. One by one, kids nodded. "Good. And don't think I won't be keeping an eye on you guys."

Ed stood where he was until Mike and his buddies backed off to the edges of the crowd.

"Hey, Madison," I heard Mike growl. "Did you bring my jacket?"

Ed watched them for a few moments before melting into the darkness.

"Is it true?" Ashleigh asked. "Do you work for Goran?"

"I helped him sell vegetables at the market this morning. Mike and his friends showed up and destroyed the stall and the produce. What does he have against the Gorans? What does everyone have against them?"

"*Them*?" she asked. "There's more than one?"

"Mr. Goran's son is in town. He's the one I was helping."

Ashleigh shook her head. "If you want to fit in around here, maybe you should stay away from him."

"You mean Mike?"

"I mean Goran. People don't like him."

"*Most* people don't like him," Charlie corrected. "And even that's an overstatement. The Winters and their friends don't like him."

"The Winters?" I said. "There was a Winters Farm stall at the market."

Ashleigh nodded. "That's them."

"What do they have against Mr. Goran?"

"You haven't heard?"

"Well, I know Mr. Goran—the father, not the son—bought the farm from Mr. Winters. And Mr. Winters told Mr. Goran's son that Mr. Goran stole the farm. But that's it."

"That's exactly it," Ashleigh said. "Ted Winters's family has farmed in this area since the mid-1800s. Up until two years ago, his father, Clyde, was farming the same land his great-grandfather cleared and planted way back when. I don't know much about farming, but I do know that there are good years and bad years. Sometimes the bad years have to do with the weather, and sometimes they have to do with things like prices and subsidies. My dad tried to explain it to me, but it's complicated."

"All you really need to know is that Clyde had a bunch of bad years in a row," Charlie said. "And that they couldn't have come at a worse time."

"What do you mean?"

"He'd loaned Ted a lot of money for new equipment. Then there were a couple of drought years. At the same time, Clyde decided to change his crop mix— that turned out to be a bad decision. He'd taken out a second mortgage on his place to get the equipment for Ted, and then he started losing money because of the new crop. Finally, the bank foreclosed on him and put the farm up for auction."

"So what's the big deal?"

"The big deal is that the auction wasn't supposed to turn out the way it did."

"Wasn't *supposed* to?" I said. "Who knows how an auction is supposed to turn out? It turns out the way it turns out—the highest bidder wins."

"Boy, do you ever not understand Moorebridge!" Ashleigh shook her head again. "Ted felt terrible that his father was going to lose the farm on his account. He didn't have the money to bail out Clyde. So instead he organized the other farmers in the area—they're a pretty tight bunch, especially the old-timers. He got everyone to put up some money to help buy Clyde's farm. It wasn't a lot from each person, but altogether it would meet the reserve bid—"

"Reserve bid?"

"The bank set a minimum price for the farm. That's the reserve bid."

"Oh."

"But a couple of other people showed up at the auction who weren't supposed to be there," Charlie said.

"Like Mr. Goran?" I asked.

"If you ask me, Ted should have talked to him and explained the situation," Charlie said. "Maybe he didn't think Mr. Goran could outbid them. But he did. You should have seen the look on Ted's face."

"You were there?"

Charlie nodded.

"How does Mike fit into this?"

"Clyde was his grandfather."

"Was?"

"He died six months after he lost his farm at auction," Charlie said. "Car accident."

"*Single-car* accident," Ashleigh said in an ominous voice. "Ted's brother-in-law tried to hush it up, but my dad knows the doctor who did the autopsy. Apparently Clyde had been drinking, and his car went off the road. Ted says it happened because his dad was depressed after losing the farm. He blames Mr. Goran."

"All Mr. Goran did was show up at a public auction," I said. "He just wanted a farm. He'd wanted one ever since he left Kurdistan."

"He just happened to pick the wrong farm in the wrong town," Ashleigh said.

"And I guess farming here isn't the same as farming in Kurdistan," Charlie added.

"What do you mean?"

"Well, he burned down his barn to collect the insurance money, didn't he? So the place must have been in trouble."

"Maybe he didn't do it."

Both Charlie and Ashleigh looked at me as if I were a hopelessly muddled newcomer.

"You said Ted Winters's brother-in-law tried to hush up the autopsy results," I said. "So the Winters family must have a lot of influence around here."

"Not really. But Brian's a cop, just like—" Ashleigh caught herself and stopped abruptly. She'd been going to say just like my aunt.

Brian? "Brian Shears?" I asked.

"Don't tell me you know him too," Ashleigh said.

"I met him at the market this morning. He's Mike's uncle?"

Ashleigh nodded.

No wonder he hadn't been overly keen to find out who had trashed Aram's stall.

We stayed at the party until well after midnight, which is when Ashleigh started yawning.

"I did a ten-hour shift today," she said. "It's catching up with me. You ready to go?"

I was.

Charlie looked disappointed.

"Relax, Romeo," Ashleigh said. "She's spending the night at my house. She's not leaving town. You two can get together another time."

"Can we?" Charlie asked me shyly.

Suddenly I felt just as shy. He was cute. He was fun. And he was spunky enough to have taken on Mike Winters.

"Sure," I said. "You know where I live."

We said goodnight and walked back along the beach to Ashleigh's house, where we settled down for the night. I called Aunt Ginny, who promised to drop off my bike the next morning so I could get back home—she had to work. Ashleigh was snoring softly almost as soon as her head hit the pillow. I lay awake wondering what would happen when I went to the police station to try to press charges against Mike Winters for trashing Mr. Goran's stall. I wondered too how it might affect Aunt Ginny, who was doing her best to get accepted.

EIGHT

Ashleigh's parents were welcoming and unobtrusive, and her mother was a great cook. She made waffles for breakfast, with maple syrup and fresh fruit.

Aunt Ginny arrived exactly when she said she would and insisted on meeting the Wainwrights. They welcomed her as warmly as they had me and offered her breakfast. Aunt Ginny looked longingly at the waffles and genuine maple syrup and sniffed the freshly brewed coffee even more longingly. But she glanced at her watch and said, "I have to be on duty in five minutes."

"Oh. Are you a nurse?" Mrs. Wainwright asked.

A look of annoyance flickered across Aunt Ginny's face.

"Police officer," she said. "Detective."

"How interesting," Mrs. Wainwright said. "You and Riley will have to come to supper sometime, and you can tell us all about it."

Aunt Ginny looked at the waffles again. Although she was a terrible cook, she had an eye for expertly prepared food, so I'm sure she relished the prospect of dining with the Wainwrights. What she would never relish, however, was discussing her job with a couple of mere civilians. I wondered if it would deter her from accepting an invitation.

I thanked Ashleigh's parents and left with Aunt Ginny. She started to unload my bike from the back of her car, but I stopped her.

"I need to go to the police station first," I said.

"What for?"

"I want to get someone charged with…" What would be the proper charge? Vandalism? Destruction of property?

"With what?" Aunt Ginny's eyes narrowed. "Did something happen at that party last night?"

"No."

"Riley?" She wasn't going anywhere until I answered her, even if it meant she would be late for work.

I told her about meeting Mike Winters and that he was the ringleader for what had happened at the market.

Aunt Ginny sighed. "You should talk to Brian Shears. He took your report, didn't he? Let him arrest this boy."

"I don't think he'll do it."

"Why not?"

"Because he's Mike Winters' uncle."

Aunt Ginny gave me a sharp look.

"Are you saying you don't think a police officer will do his job because his nephew is involved?"

"He didn't take me seriously when I reported the incident. I bet he knew it was Mike."

"He's a cop. He'll do his job. But you're not the person to lay charges. It was Aram's property. He should do it."

"Okay. So let's call him."

"Riley, I don't know if you understand what's going on here, but from what I gather, the Gorans aren't exactly in the running for neighbors of the year. There's a lot of resentment against them."

"So?"

She shook her head. "So nothing, I guess." But the reluctance in her voice made me wonder. "We'll call Aram from the station."

We drove to the police station, and I followed Aunt Ginny inside. I spotted Brian Shears almost immediately. He wasn't in uniform. Aunt Ginny called to him.

"*Detective* McFee." There was something grating about the way he emphasized her rank, as if he were mocking her. "Who have you got here?" He shifted his eyes to me. "Well, if it isn't the girl from the market. Did you have any luck tracking down the alleged vandal?"

"She did," Aunt Ginny informed him.

Shears's gaze flicked back to Aunt Ginny. "Moving up from kittens and puppies, Detective?"

"Riley is my niece, *Constable.*" Aunt Ginny could give as good as she got.

"So I hear."

"And apparently your nephew is the one who vandalized the Gorans' market stall. Riley can positively identify him."

"I'd love to help, but I'm off duty today, Detective. You'll have to stick-handle this yourself. Have a great day, ladies."

As he left the squad room, Aunt Ginny muttered something under her breath. "Come on," she said. She led me to a desk and logged in to her computer. After a glance at the screen, she picked up the phone and dialed. "Mr. Goran?"

I listened as she explained why she was calling. Then there was silence as she listened to Aram.

"You're sure?" she asked finally. More silence. "Okay. It's your decision." She hung up. "That's that," she said. "Let's get your bike unloaded so I can get to work."

"What happened?"

"He doesn't want to press charges."

"Why not?"

"Because, as I said, there's been enough bad blood around here already without him pressing charges against Ted Winters' son."

"But—"

"I'm just telling you what he said, Riley."

"So Mike gets away with being a bully and destroying other people's property?"

"It was Aram's property. So it's his decision how to proceed. He doesn't want to press charges. There's nothing I can do." I followed her out to the parking lot, where she unloaded my bike. "I don't know if I want you getting too involved with the Gorans."

I couldn't believe what she was saying. "Why not?"

"There's been enough trouble. Besides, it doesn't look like they're going to be around for much longer. If Mr. Goran survives and manages to dodge jail, it's doubtful he'll be able to go back to farming. And I'm sure Aram has a life to get back to. You and I, however, have to live in this town."

"Are you worried about what people will think?"

"I didn't say that."

"Aram didn't commit any crime. Mike did."

She set my bike onto the pavement. "It's quite possible Aram's father did too. A serious one. And Aram's not going to be here for much longer. I don't see any reason to get involved in a situation that is so heated and so temporary." She handed me my lock. "I'll see you at supper."

I didn't go home right away. Instead, I dug out my cell phone and looked up Charlie's home phone number. He sounded surprised to hear from me.

"Do you want to meet up for a coffee or something?" I asked.

"How about ice cream? I'll meet you at Chuck's. It's next to the pharmacy on King Street." King Street was the main commercial street.

Charlie got there before me. He beamed when he saw me but was disappointed when I opted for a soda instead of an ice-cream cone or a sundae.

"Ashleigh's mom made waffles," I explained. "I think I ate one too many."

We sat on a bench outside Chuck's.

"Charlie, what do you know about the Gorans and the Winters?"

Charlie slumped a little. "I thought you wanted to see me."

"I did. I do. I called you, didn't I? But if Mike Winters is going to give me a hard time, I want to know everything about him."

"Besides the fact that he's a jerk?"

"Yeah, besides that."

"Well, Mr. Goran bought the farm nearly two years ago, but Mike and his dad still haven't gotten over it. Whenever Ted sees Mr. Goran in town, he makes a point of crossing the street to avoid him. Mike does the opposite. He doesn't avoid Mr. Goran. He accidentally-on-purpose bumps into him, hard if Mr. Goran is carrying something. He keyed Mr. Goran's truck a couple of times—"

"You saw him do that?"

Charlie shook his head. "He boasted about it at school. He makes fun of Mr. Goran's accent. He calls him names. He's knocked over the old man's mailbox a couple of times."

"Did he ever get arrested for any of that stuff?"

"Not that I know of." Charlie bit into his ice-cream cone. "Anyway, Mr. Goran seems okay. He sure works hard. And he knows what he's doing."

"What do you mean?"

"We have a fall fair up here every year. There are a lot of competitions—baking, needlecrafts, livestock and produce. All the entries are anonymous, you know, so the judges can't be influenced by whether they know someone or not. Mr. Goran won a bunch of prizes last year. I think he got firsts for his beets, his tomatoes and his squash. And he won first for his oats in the grain category. The tourists who were there—

we always get a lot of city people—they all clapped. But people in town? No way." He paused to pop the last bit of his ice-cream cone into his mouth.

"People up here sure carry a grudge," I said. "It must have been hard for Mr. Goran. I've seen his place. It seems big for one person to run alone. Did he have anyone working with him?"

"There was a guy out there for a while. I think he was from the same place as Mr. Goran. They spoke the same language. But I heard he went back home to get married. That was during the winter. Mr. Goran put up some notices around town—he wanted to hire help for the growing season. I think he took out an ad in the paper too."

"And?"

"He didn't get anyone."

"But there must be plenty of people who need work," I said. The news was filled with grim statistics on unemployment.

"You're not kidding. I sure could use some extra money."

"You should have asked him for a job."

Charlie's face flushed red. He crumpled the napkin he had been holding and glanced at his watch. "I gotta go."

"Already? But I have more questions."

He stood up. "What does it matter? He's not going to farm anymore. That's what everyone's saying. *If he even lives.*" His voice was hard and dismissive. He sounded like a different person. He sounded like Mike Winters.

"What's the matter, Charlie?" Something was bothering him, Something had changed.

"Nothing. I gotta go." A couple of minutes ago, he'd been happy to see me. Now he couldn't wait to get away.

"Was it something I said?"

"See you around." He strode down the street. I stayed put.

He stopped at the first intersection he came to, even though he had a green light, and hung there for a few moments.

He turned.

He looked at me.

He walked back slowly and dropped down beside me on the bench.

"I like you," he said.

"It's kinda hard to tell, the way you walked off."

"I like the way you stood up to Mike."

"You stood up to him too."

"And I like the way you seem to care about Mr. Goran."

"He's a nice man," I said.

"That makes me feel even worse about what I did," Charlie said. He looked down at the ground.

"What do you mean?"

"I never told anyone."

I waited.

"It's about Mr. Goran," he finally said.

I had figured that out already.

"We had to do fundraising last year for a school project to buy livestock for families in developing countries. You know, so much money will buy a goat, and a goat can provide milk for a whole family. Stuff like that. There was a prize for the team that raised the most money. A trip to the city, a hotel right downtown, tickets to the museum."

"And?"

"I figured that Mr. Goran would be a good person to ask. He's from a developing country, and he's a farmer. He would know how much a goat or some chickens would mean to a poor family. So I asked him, and he gave me a hundred dollars—cash! That's way more than I got from anyone else. It's more than anyone else on my team collected." He paused and chanced a peek at me. "You're going to think I'm such a jerk when I tell you the rest."

I thought about all the stupid things I had done— and all the times my grandpa Jimmy had either found out or I had confessed. There were so many things about Jimmy that I missed. He had a great sense of humor. He was kind to everyone. He loved to perform, and he did it well. But most of all, he had an attitude to life that made more sense than anything I'd ever heard from anyone else. It could be summed up in two sentences, both of which I'd heard Jimmy say on many occasions. The first was *Who are we to judge?* The second: *We all have things we regret saying or doing, but we can't unsay them or undo them; the best we can do is resolve not to say them or do them again when the opportunity presents itself.* It was this outlook that made Jimmy the greatest person I'd ever known.

"Nobody's perfect, Charlie."

He offered me a sad, crooked smile before he started talking.

"When I brought the money back to my team, they wanted to know how I'd managed to raise so much.

Like an idiot, I told them it was from Mr. Goran. I thought people would like that. I mean, he already owned the farm, and Clyde Winters was dead. None of that was going to change. I thought maybe people would get over it if they saw that Mr. Goran wasn't a bad guy."

"But it didn't turn out that way, huh?"

"Uh-uh. The team had a big debate on whether to accept the money or not. Some people wanted to take it because it would guarantee that we'd win the prize. Some people didn't want it because it came from Mr. Goran. We couldn't agree, so we voted on it."

"And?"

"*I* voted to keep it. So did three other members of the team. Only two people voted against it."

"Majority rules."

"Yeah," Charlie said. "But when the grand totals raised by each team were announced, ours was a hundred dollars short. We came second by nearly fifty dollars."

"What happened to Mr. Goran's money?"

Charlie's expression soured. "A funny thing," he said. "It vanished. I asked our team treasurer, who, by the way, was one of the two people who voted against taking Mr. Goran's money, but…Once the winner was announced, nobody on my team cared anymore, not even the ones who voted with me. But that's not the whole story." Shame crept into his face again. "When I got the donation from Mr. Goran, he was really nice to me. He invited me in for tea. He asked about my family and told me about his. He seemed like a good guy. I told people that." He stared down at the ground. "Anyway, he offered me a job. He said he needed another pair of hands." He glanced at me. "I wanted to take it. He was paying more than I could make at a fast-food place or working retail. Those are the only places that hire kids. But I had to ask my folks."

"And they said no?"

"Not exactly." He crumpled the napkin he'd been holding. "They said it was too bad the way everyone was acting about Mr. Goran, but if I wanted to take the job, it was okay with them. They also told me that it might not be easy for me if I did. My mom grew up here. She was the most worried. She said people here have a certain way of looking at things and that it's hard for them to change. Once they made up their minds that Mr. Goran stole Clyde's place, they would never accept him. I knew she didn't want me to work for him. My dad said I should follow my conscience."

Again I waited. There were some things that couldn't be rushed—that *shouldn't* be rushed.

"So I didn't take it," Charlie said.

"Mr. Goran must have been disappointed."

He hung his head. "I guess."

He *guessed*? "What did he say when you told him?"

"I never did." He refused to look at me. I assumed if he didn't hear back from me that he's figured it out. And I was ashamed, you know? I wanted the job, but I didn't take it because I was afraid of what kids would think and how much I'd get hassled. I didn't tell anyone besides my parents that he'd offered to hire me. I don't think they told anyone either."

Once again I didn't know what to say. There was nothing to say. Charlie knew what he'd done and what he wished he *had* done. He didn't need me to tell him.

"The worst thing," Charlie said, "was that I started avoiding him. Once I saw him coming down the street and I crossed to the other side. I didn't think he'd noticed me. But when I glanced back, he was looking at me. You should have seen the look on his face. He was so sad, like he thought I was the same as everyone else." His eyes were watery. "He was right."

NINE

We sat in silence.

"Everybody does things they regret, Charlie," I said finally. "All you can do is apologize—"

"If I ever get the chance."

"I bet the next time something like that comes up, you'll act differently."

"Yeah." He didn't sound convinced. But he felt so bad about what he'd done that I knew I was right. Next time, he'd act in a way that made him feel better, not worse.

"You want to talk to my cousin Rick?" he asked.

I'd never even heard of his cousin Rick. "Do I?"

"He's a member of the volunteer fire department. He responded to the fire at Mr. Goran's place. He knows as much as anyone about what happened that night."

In that case, I definitely wanted to talk to him.

Rick Grenier was in his mid-twenties. He lived in an apartment above a used-book-and-music store and worked as a garage mechanic. According to Charlie, he had applied to a firefighter program at community college.

"He wants to get a job with a big-city fire department," Charlie said.

Rick's program didn't start until after Christmas, so in the meantime he was working and saving as much money as he could. We found him tinkering with an old truck that had clearly seen better days. He was happy to take a break, especially when Charlie handed him a frosty soda. He appraised me as he took a gulp.

"You're that girl," he said. "You gave a buddy of mine quite a scare when he saw you lying on the ground. He thought you were dead. So, how can I help you?"

"I want to know about the fire."

Rick polished off his soda, crumpled the can and tossed it into a recycling bin. "There's not much to tell. By the time we got there, we knew we weren't going to be able to save the barn. It was too far gone. But his animals—he had a cow and a couple of goats—were safe in a pasture across the road. Right there, I was suspicious."

"What do you mean?"

"It was nighttime, and the animals were outside. Plus the owner, Goran, hadn't called the fire department. That might make a person think the fire wasn't meant to be put out."

That it had been set intentionally, he meant.

"But Mr. Goran was trapped inside the barn," I said.

"Yeah, but what was he doing in there in the first place? And how did he get trapped?"

"But you saw he *was* trapped, right?"

"Not at first. When we first got there, we didn't see anyone. Well, except you. We were dousing the barn to keep the fire from spreading. Then, as soon as water hit the barn, someone screamed. I hate to say it, but you know what I thought? I thought Goran outsmarted himself."

"What do you mean?"

"You know about the auction?"

I nodded.

"So you know that there was a lot of resentment against him. Some people didn't hesitate to show how they felt. Goran complained a couple of times about intruders. Twice he caught kids trying to sneak into his barn—once while he was in it. So he put padlocks on the inside of three of the doors, and he locks those up at night. He rigged the main door so that if you go in, it closes automatically, locking you in unless you happen to have a key for it or one of the padlocks, and it gives him a chance to call the cops." He shook his head. "The whole rig-up is totally against the fire code, by the way, and for good reason."

No wonder I'd had so much trouble with the door.

"He must have forgotten his keys when he saw the fire," I said.

"Maybe. Or maybe he dropped them when things went wrong, and he panicked."

He most certainly panicked, I thought.

"Fire is tricky," Rick said. "A person may think he's figured out all the angles, but then the fire gets out of control. In a barn full of hay and wood and feed, that's practically guaranteed to happen. The person panics and runs, maybe he trips—I don't know. But the fire is out of control, and the person—Goran, in this case— is too scared to think straight. He's lucky to be alive. But I hear it's still touch and go."

"How do they know for sure that it's arson?"

"You mean, how did the fire marshal make that determination? He found the source of the fire. It was kerosene from one of those old-fashioned lanterns, and—I'm no expert, I'm just telling you what I heard— it was deliberately smashed right next to some bales of hay. Right next to it was a flashlight. Plus, there's been some talk about him needing money. Apparently he applied for a loan at the bank. Put that together with what I already told you, and you get arson."

I couldn't imagine Mr. Goran lighting a kerosene lamp, certainly not in a wooden barn, under any circumstances, not even if he needed money for some reason.

"You said kids snuck into his barn. Do you know who?" I asked.

"All I heard was kids." Rick shook his head. "A lot of people around here don't like Goran, even though they never got to know him. That's one reason I want to get away from here. People get so stuck in seeing things one way and thinking if that's the way it's always been, then that's the way it should stay. It's like they live in the past."

"How does the fire marshal know it was Mr. Goran and not someone else who started the fire?"

"The fire marshal determines how the fire started, not who started it. The *who* is up to the cops. You'd have to talk to them."

"What is that heavenly smell?" Aunt Ginny asked when she walked through the door that night.

"Just supper," I called from the kitchen. I opened the oven door to baste what was inside.

"You didn't!" Aunt Ginny's voice was so piercing that I almost dropped my basting spoon. "You did! Oh my god, those are my favorite!"

Compared to most people, I'm a good cook. Compared to Aunt Ginny, I'm like the chef of a five-star restaurant. I have many specialties. But Aunt Ginny's favorite is the oven-roasted ribs with spiced rice, home-made creamy coleslaw and homemade biscuits that

George (the drummer in Jimmy's band) taught me to make. You need the biscuits to sop up the extra sauce.

"It'll be ready in twenty minutes, Aunt Ginny. You have time for a shower."

She was back in the kitchen nineteen minutes later, declaring that she was famished. I put the food on the table—a heaping plate for her and a smaller serving for myself. She dug in with gusto.

"That was the best meal I've ever eaten," she declared after a second helping. "I think I'm going to explode." She sat back in her chair and smiled contentedly—for about a minute. "Is there dessert?"

"There's ice cream." It had mostly melted on the way home, but it should have firmed up again in the freezer by now.

"No pie?" Aunt Ginny sounded disappointed.

"Sorry."

She pouted. "Okay. I'll have ice cream."

I scooped a couple of balls into a dish and slid it in front of her.

"Aunt Ginny, did you read the police report on the arson investigation?"

"No. I haven't been able to get my hands on it. Why?" I cleared the plates while she ate her dessert.

"Just wondering."

She put down her spoon—a bad sign. Aunt Ginny may have wished for pie, but she loves ice cream. "I know you, Riley. I also know when I'm being softened up by your cooking. Why are you so interested in that report?"

"No special reason."

"Uh-huh." She didn't believe me. "Spit it out, kiddo."

I sat down again. "Everyone assumes it was Mr. Goran who started the fire in his barn."

Aunt Ginny's eyes narrowed. "And?"

"A lot of people around here don't like him, and at least one of your colleagues is related to Ted Winters—well, to his wife. Mr. Winters claims that Mr. Goran stole the farm, and there are a lot of people who believe him."

"Brian Shears is a patrol officer, not an investigator. He has nothing to do with the arson investigation."

"Who handled that? Who decided that Mr. Goran was the perpetrator?"

"It's Josh's case."

"Is Josh related to Ted Winters in any way?"

"Not that I know of. If he was, presumably he wouldn't be on the case."

"Presumably?"

"It's a small town, Riley. Being related shouldn't make a difference to a good detective."

"How do you know how good a detective is?"

"By how well he or she does the job—" Aunt Ginny sat back in her chair. "Oh no you don't."

"No I don't what?"

"I just got here, Riley. They're nowhere near finished hazing me yet. There's no way I'm going to make things any worse right now, which means there's no way I'm going to start second-guessing my own boss before I earn his respect and trust. I worked hard to get this job. Once I get over this initiation period, I'll be fine. And if I do a good job here, I'll be able to move to a larger police service. I don't want to mess this up. And I sure don't want you to mess it up for me."

"But what if Mr. Goran isn't the arsonist?"

"It's not my case, Riley. There's no way I'm getting involved. Not unless you have something solid, which you don't and you are not going to have, ever, because *you're* not getting involved either."

"But what if it wasn't him? It could have been one of his enemies, like Mr. Winters. He hates Mr. Goran."

"I said proof, not conjecture. I can't afford to be seen as a flake or, worse, as an overly competitive female who strolls in and right away starts telling everyone else how to do their job. Understand?"

The make-her-favorite-supper bribe wasn't working nearly as well as I'd hoped.

"Do you, Riley?"

"Yes." But I didn't. I mean, what's more important—what other people think or the truth? Personally, I was on truth's side and didn't care what other people thought, especially if it turned out that one or more of them were the real arsonists.

"And I don't want to hear anything more about that fire," she added.

I cleaned up the kitchen while Aunt Ginny silently finished her ice cream.

TEN

Charlie was red-faced and breathless when I answered the door the next morning. Ashleigh was with him, drenched in sweat. Their bicycles were leaning against the porch.

"What's going on?" I asked.

"Water," Charlie croaked.

"Mr. Martial Arts needs more cardio." Ashleigh laughed and nodded at Charlie.

I brought them inside and gave them something cold to drink. Charlie collapsed in a chair, took a few gulps and then held his glass against his forehead.

"So?" I prodded.

Ashleigh pulled a folded sheet of paper from her pocket, unfolded it and handed it to me.

"This was posted on the notice board at work."

It was a Help Wanted ad. I skimmed it.

"And?"

"I went in to get some things for my mom," Charlie said. "I saw Madison tear that off the bulletin board and throw it in the garbage. She looked so mad, I got curious. I thought we could apply."

The help was wanted by Aram. He was advertising for people to pick his father's berry crop.

"Did you call the number?" I asked. Then: "We?"

"He's too chicken to do it alone." Ashleigh said. "He wants you to go with him."

"Aram doesn't bite," I said.

"Please? Maybe his dad said something to him about me. If you come with us, it'll be easier. Plus, I thought you might want a job too. We could work together."

"We could all work together," Ashleigh said. "I only have three shifts at the store this week. I could use the extra money."

If it would help Aram, I was all for it. We got on our bikes and rode over to the farm. Aram was thrilled that we were interested.

"There's a market up in Clarkson," he said. "I spoke to a woman up there who told me she'd be happy to sell the berries for a small commission. But I have to get them picked. It'll be a full day's work."

I introduced Ashleigh and Charlie. Charlie flinched when I said his name, as if he expected Aram to recognize it and throw him off his property. I hadn't told him that Aram and his father hadn't spoken to each other for years.

Aram welcomed Charlie and Ashleigh. He took us into the garage and gave us each a bucket.

"What are we picking?" Ashleigh asked.

"Blueberries."

She frowned. The buckets Aram had given us were large, like the kind you'd use to mop a floor. She glanced around.

"Those would be better." She pointed to smaller containers stacked on a bench. "Do you have scissors and some string?"

Mr. Goran looked puzzled but found what she wanted. Ashleigh punched holes near the rims of each container with the scissors. She cut off lengths of string, threaded them through the holes and tied them.

"If we wear these around our necks, we'll have both hands free for picking. It'll go faster." She demonstrated. "And smaller pails will stop the berries from getting crushed."

"You've done this before," Aram said with a smile.

"Only every summer," Ashleigh said. "But usually I get paid in Mom's blueberry pie or blueberry jam."

The three of us grabbed a handful of containers and set off for the blueberry patch, where Ashleigh gave us some pointers.

"Look for the round blue ones," she said. "If they're white, they haven't begun to ripen—and they never will if you pick them. If they're small and feel hard, they're sour, so leave them. Same thing if they don't come off the stem easily. And make sure the skin isn't cracked."

We started to work, each in a separate area but close enough that we could talk. I asked Ashleigh if she had heard about the break-ins at Mr. Goran's farm.

"Sure. It was Mike, every time."

"How do you know?"

"Are you kidding? He can't keep his mouth shut. If Mike comes equipped with a mute button, no one has ever found it."

"So he admitted he broke into the barn?"

"Admitted? He announced it to everyone, even if they weren't interested. He was proud of himself."

"I never heard that," Charlie said.

"That's because you're not part of his crowd."

"And you are?" I asked. That surprised me. Ashleigh seemed so nice, and Mike seemed, well, the exact opposite.

"Not me exactly. You remember Taylor? Her father is a cousin of one of Mike's uncles, so they're friendly. And Madison has a thing for Mike. So she's always pumping Taylor for information. I can't help knowing what's going on with him."

"So what's the story on the break-ins?" I asked. "Did he want to vandalize the barn?"

"Maybe, but what he really wanted are the brasses."

"Brasses?"

"Horse brasses. His grandfather had a collection of them."

"You're talking about those decorations people put on harnesses, right?" I asked.

"Right. Mike's great-grandfather used to raise heavy horses," Ashleigh said. "Raised them and bred them. He's the one who started the collection.

Supposedly it's amazing. And valuable. Did you know that horse brasses have been around for centuries?"

"No. And I'm kind of surprised you know."

"Mike gave a talk about them one year in school. He said they've been around in one form or another for over two thousand years. Lots of people collect them. And they aren't all made of brass either. Some are made of ceramic. Some are silver. There are even gold ones, although I don't think Clyde had any of those. Mike says he kept them in the barn, on harnesses hanging from the rafters."

I'd seen them the afternoon before the fire, when Mr. Goran gave me a tour of the farm. I'd wanted to ask, but at first he'd been pointing out things so enthusiastically that I didn't want to interrupt him, and then he'd been fussing and worrying about some loose boards he found that could give a fox or some other animal access to his barn. After that, I forgot about them.

"Why didn't he take them when the bank foreclosed on the place?"

"The way I heard it, everyone assumed he'd taken all his personal property off the place before the auction. That's what Taylor says anyway, and she always seems to know what's going on. She says she heard that Clyde was embarrassed about the foreclosure. He didn't say anything to anyone until the auction notices went up. That's when Mike's father found out about it. By then Clyde was living in an old trailer on a friend's place and had boxes of his stuff stored in the friend's shed. Ted didn't go through them until months after Clyde died. That's when he realized the brasses were missing."

"Missing as in stolen?"

"Missing as in Clyde had left them in the barn."

"So why didn't Mike just ask for them back?"

"The way I heard it from Taylor, the place was auctioned off as is. Whatever was on the property at the time of the auction was considered part of the sale. So if the brasses were there, Mr. Goran owned them."

"But if Ted or Mike had asked nicely…"

Ashleigh and Charlie sighed and shook their heads in unison.

"Can you really picture Mike doing *anything* nicely?" Charlie said. "Besides, by the time Ted realized that Clyde had left the brasses in the barn, the whole family had been shunning Mr. Goran for nearly a year, and Mike had been so rude that I'm sure there was no way Mr. Goran would have given him the time of day, let alone a collection of valuable brasses."

"So Mike decided to break into the barn and steal them instead?"

"He tried it twice. Mr. Goran chased him off both times, which only made Mike more determined. Mr. Goran did something to the door so that it would trap you inside. Mike was trying to figure out how to beat it. Then the fire happened."

"I wonder what happened to the brasses," I said.

Ashleigh shrugged. "Maybe they melted."

Maybe. If the fire had been hot enough, I guessed. It was something to check out.

"Has Mike mentioned them lately?" I asked.

Ashleigh's eyes narrowed. "What are you getting at, Riley? You don't think Mike started the fire, do you?"

The thought had crossed my mind. He seemed to have a motive. And if the brasses were missing, that could further point the finger at Mike. He could have figured out how to beat Mr. Goran's new lock, broken into the barn, taken back his brasses and set fire to the place. He could also have locked Mr. Goran in—accidentally or on purpose. If he had, and if Mr. Goran didn't recover, it could be the difference between manslaughter and murder.

"I sure would like to know what happened to those brasses," I said.

"You could ask Taylor's dad," Ashleigh said.

"Why? Does he know Mr. Goran?"

"He's handling the arson investigation. He would probably know if the brasses were there or if they melted or whatever."

Taylor's dad was handling the arson investigation? "You mean he's a cop?"

"Detective Sergeant Joshua Martin."

Joshua. Josh. Aunt Ginny's boss. Small world. Smaller town.

"Or you could ask Ted. He might know," Charlie said. "He must have been there that night."

"Why would Ted Winters be at the fire?"

"He's the head of the volunteer fire department."

I stared at Charlie.

"I guess I forgot to mention that, huh?" he said.

"I guess you did."

We picked blueberries all morning. While I worked, I thought about what Ashleigh had just told me. And I wondered about those brasses. Had they been in the barn when it was set on fire? If they had, and if they'd survived, where were they now? I had the feeling that might be the key to the arson. And Mike Winters was the likeliest suspect.

Maybe Ashleigh was right. Maybe I should talk to Taylor's dad. But would he tell me anything? More important, what would Aunt Ginny do if she found out I'd even tried to talk to him?

Aram came down to the blueberry patch with sandwiches and cold drinks, and we all sat in the shade of a massive oak to eat.

"You kids are doing a great job," Aram said, looking at how much we had picked. "My father would be pleased if he knew that his berries were going to the market."

"How is he?" Charlie asked.

Aram gazed over the fields that surrounded us. "It will be a long time, if ever, before he can farm again. I don't relish the job of telling him he might have to sell the place. This farm was all he ever wanted."

Charlie looked down at the half-eaten sandwich in his hand. From the somber look on his face, I guessed he was thinking about how he had treated Aram's father. I could have been wrong though.

"You seem to know your way around a farm," I said to Aram. "Maybe you could run the place for him."

He shook his head. "Despite what my father thinks, I'm happy in my work."

"Your father doesn't like what you do?"

"It makes him afraid. We can't even talk about it."

"What do you do?" Ashleigh asked.

"I work for a relief agency in Afghanistan. My father thinks I'm wasting my time and that something bad will happen to me. I was taken hostage once a few years ago by some extremists. I managed to negotiate my way out of it. It helped that I speak Pashtu. But my father was furious. He demanded I return home." He shook his head. "My father thinks I should help only myself. He thinks everyone should help themselves and then all the problems in the world would be solved."

We were all silent for a few moments. Then Ashleigh said, "I want to be a dancer. My parents say it's a good hobby, but it's not practical to think I could support myself by dancing. They push me to stay on the honor roll."

"Your parents and my father would get along," Aram said. "Except that immigrant parents are even more determined that their children should succeed—and succeeding means making lots of money. My father says that's why he moved here—to make sure that I had opportunities he never had in Kurdistan." He shook his head again. "I hate that the last time we spoke, we argued."

None of us knew what to say. The silence that followed was broken only when Aram stood up. "I'd better let you get back to work. I have some chores to attend to."

"I feel sorry for him," Ashleigh said as she watched him go. "I think he loves his father. Can you imagine how terrible he'll feel if his father dies before he can tell him that?"

We headed out into the sun to continue working. We were about to take a midafternoon break when someone called Charlie's name.

"That sounds like Rick. What's he doing here?"

"I could use a drink," Ashleigh said. "Let's take a break."

We carried our picked berries up to the shed.

"It *is* Rick." There was a second pickup parked behind Mr. Goran's in the driveway, and, sure enough,

Rick was standing beside it. Aram was standing with him. Neither was talking and both looked relieved when we appeared.

"Your mom wants you home pronto," Rick said to Charlie.

"How did you know where I was?"

"My mom said someone saw you at the supermarket with a flyer, so she called your mom, and…" He glanced apologetically at Aram, whose face remained expressionless. "She sent me to get you."

"But I'm working," Charlie protested. "Mom's been bugging me all summer to earn some money so I don't have to ask her every time I want something."

"Hey, I'm just the messenger, so there's no point arguing with me. All I know is that if I go back without you I'm going to have both your mom and mine on my back. You don't want that, do you? Because I sure don't."

Charlie fumbled in his pocket for his cell phone. He pulled it out, looked at it as if he was contemplating making a call and then slipped it back into his shorts pocket. "I'd better go," he said at last.

"Atta boy," Rick said.

"I came on my bike."

"Get it, and I'll throw it in the back of the truck." While Charlie retrieved his bike, Rick turned to Aram. "I'm sorry about your father, Mr. Goran."

"Aram. My name is Aram."

Rick nodded. "I hope he recovers. When I got here that night—"

"You were here?" Aram regarded him with new interest.

"I'm a volunteer firefighter. I was on my way to Clarkson, but I turned the truck around as soon as I got the call. By the time I got here, the rest of the crew was doing everything they could, but by then the place was lighting up the sky." He shook his head. "I think that's why Ted didn't hear at first. Either that or he thought his ears were playing tricks on him."

"Ted?" Aram said.

"Ted Winters. Our fire chief. He was on a hose when I got there. I went to spell him. That's when I heard it too."

"I don't think I understand. Heard what?" Aram asked.

Rick looked flustered. "Your father. The screaming." He broke off again. "Look, I'm sorry. I shouldn't have said that. I didn't mean to upset you. I hope your dad gets better. I really do."

"You're the person who pulled my father out of the fire?"

"Me and Ted. We did it together."

"But only after *you* arrived. And you arrived *after* Mr. Winters and some of the others."

Rick squirmed under Aram's gaze. I didn't blame him. Maybe he'd thought Aram knew everything that happened that night. But one thing he had not known was that someone—Ted Winters—had heard his father screaming inside the barn and done nothing to help him. That was news to me too. And it made me wonder, how could Ted not have heard something that Rick said he heard clearly? Maybe Ted had only pretended not to hear the screams. Maybe he'd hoped no one else would hear them either. I added Ted to my list of suspects.

Rick seemed relieved when Charlie wheeled his bike over. It gave him an excuse to break free of Aram's scrutiny and load the bike into the bed of the pickup.

"I'll call you later, okay?" Charlie said to me. He looked at Aram. "I'm sorry I have to go."

"I haven't paid you yet," Aram said. "I was going to go to the bank."

"You can give it to Riley for me." Charlie climbed into the truck's cab. Rick got in behind the wheel. He didn't make eye contact as he backed out of the drive.

Ashleigh and I resumed picking. Aram drove into town. When we finally knocked off for the day, Aram presented us with small brown pay envelopes. Ashleigh said she would drop Charlie's off on her way home. She peeked into her envelope and grinned broadly at what she saw.

"Thanks, Mr. Goran! Any time you need any more help, just let me know."

He smiled. "You have lived here a long time, correct?" Ashleigh nodded. "Do you know where this Ted Winters lives?"

Uh-oh.

Ashleigh glanced at me. What could I say?

"Please," Aram said.

I guess she figured that if she didn't tell him, someone else would. She told him what he wanted to know. I told myself that Aram just wanted more information about the fire. But I wasn't sure I believed it.

ELEVEN

When I went back to Mr. Goran's farm the next morning, Aram was standing in the driveway, staring at something he was turning over and over in his hand.

"Is everything okay?" I asked.

He held up the object he had been handling. It was a key chain with a metal tag attached to it and a set of keys hanging from it.

"The tag used to be enameled," he said. "But the enamel was ruined by the fire. It was the flag of Kurdistan. The fire marshal found the keys. He said they were on the floor in front of a door that was padlocked.

He says he thinks my father tried to get out that way first, but he must not have been able to find the right key. Or he dropped them and couldn't find them again and then panicked and decided to try the main door."

Any of the things he mentioned were too horrible to contemplate. I didn't know what to say. As it turned out, I wouldn't have had time to say anything anyway, because two cars turned in to the driveway. One was a police squad car. The other was an unmarked car with Aunt Ginny at the wheel.

Aunt Ginny and the two cops got out of their cars. Aunt Ginny led the way to where Aram and I were standing. She did not look pleased to see me.

"Step away, Riley," she said.

"Why? What's the matter?"

"Step away." She all but barked the words at me. I stepped away. "Aram Goran, you are under arrest for aggravated assault."

"What?" I was stunned.

Aunt Ginny didn't look at me. She nodded at the two officers, who approached Aram and handcuffed him.

"You are making a mistake," Aram said. "I didn't assault anyone."

"You were seen in an altercation with Ted Winters in town last evening. There were dozens of witnesses. You were also spotted fleeing from his barn after dark, immediately after he was badly beaten. You'd better hope his condition improves, or you could be facing a murder charge."

I was stunned. "Aunt Ginny, you can't be serious."

"Take him in," Aunt Ginny said to the two patrol officers. I watched them march Aram to the squad car and tuck him into the back. "I'll see you at home later," Aunt Ginny said to me before she climbed back into her own car. They drove away.

It didn't take the local news long to get hold of the arrest story and to start spewing out details.

There had been nearly twenty people at the Sip 'n' Bite during the supper rush, a good portion of them with a clear view of the street. Some of those patrons told a local news reporter that they'd seen Aram Goran stop Ted Winters in the street and have what appeared to be a "heated argument" that ended with Ted stalking away and Aram staring after him with what one woman described as "murder in his eyes."

Ted's wife, Cindy, filled in the subsequent chain of events. She said Aram had come to their farm the previous night and that he and Ted had another argument. She said she almost called the police because "it looked like it was going to get physical." She went outside with the phone in her hand. When Aram saw her, he left. Later that night, Ted thought he heard something and went outside to investigate. When he didn't come back, his wife went out to look for him. She said she must have surprised his attacker, because she heard footsteps running away. She found Ted unconscious and bleeding in the barn. She ran after the assailant, but all she saw were his taillights disappearing down the road. She said she was sure Aram Goran—she was positive it was him—would have killed Ted if she hadn't shown up when she did. The reporter finished by saying that Ted Winters had been unable to identify his assailant.

I shut off the TV.

The whole situation was crazy. Aram's father had been accused of stealing Clyde Winters's farm when all he had done was make the highest bid at a public auction. Mike Winters had broken into Mr. Goran's barn at least twice. Now Aram was under arrest for attacking Clyde's son. This had all the makings of a family feud. If only I'd obeyed Aunt Ginny that night! I would have seen the fire a lot sooner. I could have saved Mr. Goran. Maybe I would even have seen who set the fire. Everything would be different.

I still didn't believe that Aram's father had burned down his own barn. It didn't make any sense. Aram didn't believe it either. He had said as much. And since it had been ruled arson, he probably thought the same thing I did, that someone with a grudge against his father had done it. Clearly, he had decided on Ted Winters as his number-one suspect. Aram must have had nerves of steel to talk his way out of a hostage situation. He had to be tough, too, to do the kind of work he did in one of the most troubled places on earth. But would he really have beaten up Ted Winters? Was he that kind of person?

I rode into town and went straight to the garage where Charlie's cousin Rick worked.

"If you're looking for Charlie," he said, glancing at me from under the hood of a vintage Chevy, "he's at home. I heard he's grounded."

"Grounded? For being at the Gorans' place?"

"His mom's not about to back down, not after what happened last night."

"You mean Ted Winters?"

He nodded. "Cindy told the cops that fellow Aram did it."

"I read that Ted couldn't identify his attacker."

"I don't know another soul in town who'd want to beat Ted Winters almost to death. I think you're going to be lucky if Charlie is allowed to see you again."

"Me? What did I do?"

"You got him involved out there."

That wasn't true. Picking berries had been Charlie's idea. But I wasn't about to tell Rick that. It might get Charlie into more trouble.

"By that logic, you're as much to blame as I am. You're the one who got Aram all worked up about Ted Winters," I said.

"Me?"

"You told him that you were the one who heard his father screaming. You. Not Ted, who was there before you. He might have wondered if Ted just pretended not to hear anything."

"And that gives him the right to attack Ted?"

"Of course not." I couldn't help shaking my head. "The first time I met you, you said you couldn't wait to leave town because of the way everyone thinks around here. But you sound just like everyone else."

"I have nothing against the father. Maybe he burned down his own place, and maybe he didn't. But this thing with Ted is different. A lot of people saw him and Aram arguing. It was heated."

I wasn't going to convince him of Aram's innocence without some hard proof. But that wasn't why I was here.

"Can I ask you something, Rick?"

He thought about it for a few seconds before saying, "Shoot."

"What happens if there's a fire but the volunteers aren't at home or at work to answer the call?"

He probably wondered why I was asking, but if he did, he didn't say anything. "In the old days, they used to ring a bell, and whoever heard it would show up. After that, they'd call you at home. These days it's all done by cell phone." Rick patted the back pocket of his overalls. "You get the call. You say where you are and give an ETA—estimated time of arrival—and we get the truck out as fast as we can with whoever turns up first."

"And you weren't home when you got the call?"

"I was on my way up to Clarkson to see my girlfriend. That's why I got there late."

"What about Ted Winters?"

"What about him?"

"Where was he when he heard about the fire?"

"I heard one of the guys say he was out at the cemetery. He's out there pretty regular, but this particular night, the night of the fire, would have been Clyde's seventy-fifth birthday. Ted was there when he got the call."

"At the cemetery."

"Look, I know you and Goran are neighbors, and I can see you're friendly with his son. I also know that your aunt is a police officer. But that doesn't give you license to cause trouble for people like Ted. He's a good man. I've known him my whole life. That Aram fella deserves to be locked up for a long time for what he did last night. And anyone who thinks Ted had anything to do with that fire doesn't deserve much better."

Clyde Winters was buried behind a sturdy brick Presbyterian church at the west end of town, nearly five miles from Ted Winters's farm. And when I say the end of town, I mean the very end, past the last of the houses, with nothing around it but fields and stands of trees—windbreaks, for the most part. If Ted Winters had been at the cemetery the night of the fire, his truck would have been parked nearby. But would anyone have seen it way out here? Could anyone confirm where he'd been?

I circled the church and walked into the cemetery, where I wandered among the headstones. Some of them dated to the time of the town's settlement over 150 years ago. Among the older stones were little ones laid flat on the ground, marking the resting places of babies and small children who never had the chance to grow up. Those stones made me sad.

"Can I help you?" a voice asked.

A grizzled and sunbaked old man squinted at me from under the brim of a straw hat. He was holding the handles of a wheelbarrow that contained a rake, a hoe and a shovel.

"I'm looking for Clyde Winters' grave."

The man released his grip on the wheelbarrow handles and studied me before answering. "You're not one of Clyde's grandchildren."

"No, I'm not."

"Then if you don't mind my asking, what do you want with his grave?"

"I'm new in town," I said. "I've heard a lot about Mr. Winters. I live next door to his old farm."

"The Carter house." The old man nodded. "Hank Carter was a good friend of mine. A good poker player. If he had a tell, I never found it."

I knew all about tells. The guys in Jimmy's band and the roadies played poker regularly. They were always looking for each other's tells, those little gestures or rituals that could tip off other players to a person's hand.

"I didn't know Alison had sold that house," the old man said.

"We're renting it."

The old man rubbed his chin. "Clyde, now he was a terrible poker player. You could read his face like you could read a book, not that you'd ever convince him of that. He thought he had a solid poker face. He never understood why he lost as often as he did. Good thing he was a better farmer than he was a card player. His grave's in the back, under that big oak." He nodded at a massive tree in the distance with strong, broad branches. "All the Winters are buried back there. Have been since the town was founded. I'm heading back that way. I'll show you."

He gripped the wheelbarrow handles, and I fell into step beside him. As we walked, he told me about some of the local notables who were buried in the cemetery. Most had been early settlers, and it was interesting to hear about them and how they had died. A cholera epidemic back in the 1800s had claimed a lot of lives, as had terrible accidents and childhood diseases easily preventable today. At one time, an alarming number of women died in childbirth. But that changed as the decades passed.

"Here we are," he said when we reached the very back of the cemetery. The enormous oak was surrounded by a small white-picket fence. All the gravestones inside bore the name Winters. Clyde's was the largest and newest.

I looked around. There was nothing but field and forest as far as I could see. Both the church and road were invisible from here, obstructed by trees, a mausoleum and some high hedges. There was a gravel road on the other side of the wrought-iron fence that surrounded the cemetery, and the fence had a gate in it about eleven yards from the oak tree. There was no lock on the gate.

"Where does that road go?" I asked.

"Up to a concession road. If you go far enough, up to the highway."

"Do funeral processions come in this way?"

"Processions come in through the front gates. It's prettier. More dignified. That gate there is for equipment trucks. People don't want to see them coming in the front. Some visitors come in that way too—folks whose loved ones are at rest back here in the shade." He looked up at the branches of the majestic tree. "When I go, I want to be planted under a tree so it's nice and cool for whoever comes to visit. Of course, that's assuming there's anyone left who will want to come and visit. Me and Emma, we never did have any kids. So it's Emma, and then I guess it's no one." He sighed. "Well, I have to get back to work. Anything else I can do for you?"

"Does anyone come to visit Mr. Winters?"

"Sure. His son. His grandson."

"Do they come often?"

"Often enough, I guess. Ted—that's the son—is here regular."

I pretended to study Clyde Winters' stone. "My grandpa is buried in Texas," I said. That was true. "I always visit him on his birthday." That part wasn't. I hadn't been to Jimmy's grave since the funeral. All of a sudden I wished I could go there now. I wished I could talk to him. More than that—my heart ached with missing him.

"Well, I don't know if Clyde's son or grandson does that."

"His birthday was two weeks ago," I said, reading the stone. Just as Charlie's cousin Rick had said, the fire had happened on Clyde Winters' seventy-fifth birthday. Was that what had prompted it? Had Ted or Mike or both of them thought about Clyde on that significant anniversary, nursed their grudge against Mr. Goran and decided to take action?

"Did you see Mr. Winters here?" I asked the old man. "Or his son Mike?"

"If they were, I don't suppose I'd know. I'm not back here every day. And Ted, he has a habit of coming in through that gate there."

That was interesting. So even if he had been here the night of the fire, it was probable that no one had seen him come or go or knew how long he'd been here.

If he had been here.

I was on my way back into town when I passed a park filled with kids. The smaller ones were doing crafts at picnic tables under the supervision of a couple of camp counselors. I recognized one of them: Madison. Nearby, boys were kicking around a soccer ball. Mike and his friends. I was hoping to speed by unnoticed, but Mike saw me and called to me.

"Yo, new girl, wait up!" He jogged toward me. He was smiling, which is what confused me. I thought maybe he was going to apologize. I guess I also thought that if he did, I might get him to talk to me.

I got off my bike and waited.

Mike was smiling broadly when he reached me. That should have tipped me off. Should have—but didn't. He stretched out a hand. That confused me. I thought he wanted to shake and make up. Stupid, huh? Instead, he pushed me. My bike and I both fell, me on top of it.

"Hey!" I said.

"You better smarten up and stay away from those…" He used a name that if Jimmy had ever heard me say it, he would have washed my mouth out with soap. He could be old-school that way. "Or there'll be more of that for you."

"I can have you charged with assault." My voice shook with rage.

"That guy tried to kill my dad last night. I wish we had capital punishment in this country. I wish they could give him the needle."

I struggled to my feet. My knees were skinned. So were the palms of my hands. Mike's friends had drifted off the playing field and over to Mike and were now watching me. The little kids doing crafts at the picnic tables had all turned to see what the "big kids" were doing. Madison got up from one of the tables and started toward us too, but the other counselor, who looked older, called her back. Madison swung around reluctantly and sat down again, but she kept glancing in my direction.

"*If* Aram hurt your dad—and I'm not saying he did—but *if* he did, maybe it's because your father burned down his father's barn and left Aram's father inside to die."

"What? What are you talking about? My father didn't start that fire. And anyway, it isn't *his* barn. He stole it. He stole the farm from my grandfather."

He was so angry he was trembling. It made it hard for me to shake the feeling I'd had almost since meeting him.

"Were you there that night too, Mike?" I asked. "Did you help your dad? Did the two of you burn down the barn to teach him a lesson? Were you hoping to scare him away?"

Mike glowered at me. He didn't answer.

"Fine," I said.

I bent to pick up my bike. The front fender was dented.

"But just so you know, my aunt is a cop—not a patrol officer, like your uncle, but a detective. When she reopens this case"—on the day that Satan hands out ice skates in hell—"she's going to want to talk to you and your father. So I hope you have a good alibi."

"As a matter of fact, I do. I was with my friends."

I glanced at the lineup behind him. A couple of them would have made bad poker players, just like Mike's grandfather. They couldn't hide their surprise.

"Great." I was looking at them, not Mike, when I spoke. "So when my aunt questions those friends, that's what they'll say, even if it means perjuring themselves, right?" I zeroed in on the two who'd been caught off guard by Mike's claim. "So, were you with Mike that night?"

Mike glanced at them.

"You don't have to talk to her," he said. "She's not a cop. She's no one." He spun around and marched back to the playing field. His friends followed him, some a little slower than others. The two who had looked surprised glanced back over their shoulders at me.

TWELVE

According to Aunt Ginny, people aren't always what they seem. Everybody is hiding something, big or little. Everybody tells lies, even if they're little white ones. Everybody is a potential suspect until they're eliminated from the list. Every smile might be hiding black thoughts and even blacker action. Aunt Ginny has what Jimmy would have called a cynical view of the world.

Jimmy also said that people aren't always what they seem. But his take was different. He believed that most people are doing the best they can under circumstances that other people don't necessarily understand. Maybe the person walking down the street ahead of you has just lost a loved one or got bad news. Maybe the store clerk is surly because his wife has just left him, or the ill-humored lady who almost hit your car has just been diagnosed with a terminal illness. In other words, you should be kind to everyone you meet, because everyone is carrying some sort of burden. Why not be someone who gives them a smile or a kind word, who puts a little sunshine in their lives? They probably have all the storm clouds they need. No one needs any more of those. Or, as Jimmy often said, *the world doesn't need any more horses' asses.*

I preferred Jimmy's outlook. I also preferred to trust my own judgment.

There was no way someone who had worked so hard for his farm would intentionally burn down the barn, especially after what had happened to his father's farm. It made no sense to me to think otherwise. It followed logically that someone else must have done it. I had a couple of motivated suspects. But I was the only person who didn't think the arson case was as good as closed and all that remained was to see if the so-called arsonist lived or died. How was I going to prove that I was right? How was I going to turn the finger of blame away from Mr. Goran and point it at the real culprit?

My head was spinning. I didn't know where to start.

Jimmy's voice again: *Start at the beginning.*

Once upon a time there was a fire that was set intentionally.

Who set the fire?

There weren't many possibilities. I counted two, in three different scenarios—Ted Winters alone, Mike Winters alone, or Ted and Mike Winters together.

Ted had no real alibi for the night of the fire and didn't hear what Rick had heard as soon as he arrived—what I had heard before either of them got there—Mr. Goran in the barn, hammering and screaming, trying to get out. But Ted Winters couldn't tell me anything. He was in the hospital.

Mike Winters might or might not have an alibi and for sure wouldn't talk to me. Nor would his friends, although they might talk to the police if they were forced to. But that wasn't likely to happen anytime soon. Who did I know who knew Mike and might be able to tell me things about him that I didn't know?

Madison.

Madison had a thing for Mike. Taylor had said so. Madison was there when Mike and his buddies overturned Aram's table at the market. She was at the beach party, mostly hanging around with Mike. She'd definitely been interested in what had happened in the park. Maybe she also knew what Mike was doing the night of the fire.

But would she talk to me?

"Okay," Ashleigh said when I told her what I wanted. "She has a summer job at the park. We can go there on my lunch break."

I hung around outside the supermarket until Ashleigh came out, and then we walked to the park together.

"You have to do the talking," I said. "She doesn't like me."

"Sure," Ashleigh said, as if it were no big deal.

"She might think you're siding with me against her," I pointed out.

"But I'm not. I'm helping a friend." She waved at a tall and extremely good-looking guy who had a whistle on a lanyard around his neck and a clipboard tucked under one arm. "Hey, Billy, have you seen Madison?"

"She just went on break. She's probably in the locker room—the door marked *Staff Only* in the clubhouse." He pointed to a small cabin.

The clubhouse's largest room had a wall of lockers; sports equipment was neatly arranged in cubbies lining another wall. Three smaller rooms led off the main room: men's and women's washrooms and the staff locker room. Ashleigh pushed open the locker-room door before I could suggest that she knock first.

Madison was reaching into one of the lockers. She whirled around when Ashleigh burst into the room.

"Jeez, Ash! You startled me." Then she saw me. She slammed her locker shut. "What's *she* doing here?"

Ashleigh ignored the question. "We need to ask you something, Maddy."

"What?" Madison didn't take her eyes off me.

"It's about Mike."

"What about him? His father's in the hospital, you know. That guy attacked him and tried to kill him."

"It's terrible what happened to Mike's dad." Ashleigh sounded sincere—and why shouldn't she? "Just like it's terrible what happened to Mr. Goran. Imagine getting trapped in a burning barn."

Madison's eyes shifted to Ashleigh. Her expression softened for a moment. But her words didn't. "He got what he deserved. He burned down his own barn. That's what the cops are saying."

Ashleigh didn't argue with her. "How's Mike?" she asked instead. "He must be upset about his dad."

"He is. But he's glad they arrested the guy so fast."

"Maddy, I know Mike tried to break into Mr. Goran's barn a few times. He told everyone at school about it. Do you think he might have tried again the night of the fire?"

"What do you mean?" Her eyes hardened to diamond points. "You think *Mike* started the fire?"

"I didn't say that. I was just—"

"Well, he didn't. For your information, Mike was with me that night." That caught my attention, but I didn't say anything. Not then. "He didn't go anywhere near that barn. Now if you don't mind, I only have a half hour for lunch, and I'm starving." She glared at both of us but made no move to open her locker again. It was clear she wanted us gone.

Ashleigh touched Madison's arm.

"I've known you since kindergarten, Maddy. I care about you. You're my friend. And if anyone is pressuring you to do anything—"

She shook off Ashleigh's hand. "No one is pressuring me."

I nudged Ashleigh. She stared at Madison for a few more seconds before following me out of the locker room. Madison slammed the door behind us. Ashleigh stopped as soon as we were back in the main room. She held a finger to her lips and pressed her ear against the door. She stood there for a moment, frozen, before grabbing me by the arm and hustling me outside. She waited until we were far from the clubhouse before she said, "I knew it. I knew she'd call someone as soon as we left. When she's upset, she always calls someone. Except I thought it would be Taylor."

"And it wasn't?"

She shook her head. "She called Mike."

Now *that* was interesting. "Did you hear what she said?"

"It wasn't much. Just that she needs to talk to him and is going to meet him when he gets off work tonight."

"Mike has a job?"

"At the food concession at the go-kart park. It closes at eleven." She glanced at her watch. "I have to get back to work."

Eleven o'clock was a long way off. I wasn't sure I could wait. Part of me wanted to go back and shake the truth out of Madison. Was she really with Mike that night? Could she prove it? That would let him off the hook and point the finger back at his father. If I put what I had found out with what Rick had told me, I might be able to get Aunt Ginny to agree that Ted Winters had a solid reason to burn down Mr. Goran's barn.

But something nagged at me too. Mike had told me he was with friends the night of the fire. Friends, plural. Not friend, singular. And what about the two friends of his who'd looked surprised when Mike told me his alibi? What did that mean? Had they seen Mike and Madison together? Were they going to back Mike up? Or had they been surprised for another reason? I would have to wait at least until eleven o'clock to try to get an answer.

Before going home, I decided to stop by the hospital to see how Mr. Goran was doing.

The nurse on his unit was friendly.

"You're the young lady who brought flowers," she said. I still wasn't allowed to go into Mr. Goran's room, but she said I could look in on him.

There was a large window in his room that looked out onto the hospital corridor. Mr. Goran's head, chest and arms were bandaged. Maybe more of him was too, but I couldn't tell. His eyes were closed.

"Is he going to be okay?" I asked.

"He's stable, and that's good," the nurse said. "He's been awake a few times. He's not talking yet. We're not sure how much he understands or remembers."

Beneath the window were two flowering plants. One was a hibiscus with velvety red blossoms.

"His son brought that one," the nurse said. "He said his father loves flowers."

I'd never seen the second plant before. It looked like some type of bamboo, with a thatch of leaves fanning out over the tops of the stalks like a bouquet of deep green. But the thing that got me to take a second, closer look was the base of the plant. The plant was set in a shallow pot, and the stalks had been twisted somehow as they grew so that they formed an intricate pattern. I wondered how long it had taken to grow the plant.

"I'm not sure who it's from. I didn't see a card. It's called lucky bamboo. One of the orderlies recognized it. It's certainly unusual. It was delivered shortly after Mr. Goran was admitted. The last time he was awake, he saw it. He couldn't smile, but I think he was pleased."

A small sticker on the pot indicated that the plant had been bought at Carol's, where I'd bought my flowers.

By the time I left the hospital it was midafternoon, and I was starving. I locked my bike in front of the Sip 'n' Bite. The tables were all taken, so I sat on a stool at the counter and ordered a sandwich and a soda.

"Coming right up," Sharon said. "Nice to see you again, Riley."

"You remembered my name." I was flattered.

"A local celebrity like you? How could I forget?"

While I waited for my lunch, someone dashed up to the counter beside me. "I need a coffee to go, Sharon." It was Carol, from the flower shop. "And I need it fast. I have the *Back in Five Minutes* sign up."

Sharon grabbed a coffeepot and a takeaway cup.

"I was going to drop by your store after I ate," I said to Carol. "I don't know if you remember me, but—"

"Of course I do. I never forget a customer. A bright selection of fresh-cut flowers for your friend in the hospital."

"She's good," Sharon said, pouring a generous amount of cream into Carol's coffee.

"I just came from the hospital," I said. "I saw some plants of yours that were sent to Mr. Goran. A hibiscus—"

"His son sent that," Carol said. "He was very polite."

"And the other plant—the lucky bamboo—is really beautiful," I said.

"And expensive," Carol said. "The stems aren't twisted after they're grown, like some people think. The growers turn them regularly, which means they have to be constantly monitoring them. The stalks naturally lean toward the sun. It can take up to two years, depending on how complex the shape is. That's the only one I've ever sold. I had to special order it."

"It was for Deirdre, wasn't it?" Sharon handed Carol her coffee. "I saw her with it. It was so unusual that I asked her what it was called."

"That's the one. When she said it was what she wanted, I assumed it was for a client and that the bank was paying for it. But she pulled out her own credit card and said it was personal. And when I say it was expensive, Shar, I mean it cost more than a week's groceries, and you know how much those boys of hers eat."

Deduction: *If* Carol had sold only one lucky bamboo recently, *and* if Mr. Goran's plant had come from her shop, *then* this Deirdre, who presumably worked at the bank, had to be the person who had bought the plant I'd seen at the hospital.

Carol put some money on the counter. "Thanks for rushing this, Sharon. Gotta run."

"Order up" came the call from the kitchen.

Sharon fetched my sandwich and slid a soda in front of me.

"Who's Deirdre?" I asked.

"She's a loan officer at the bank. You'd think a bank would pay its employees well, since we're always hearing about the record profits they make. But James Kincaid is like every other banker—cheap with the bank's money. Poor Deirdre can barely make ends meet—she's a single mom with three growing boys."

"Order up!" The voice from the kitchen was louder this time. Grumpy too.

Sharon dashed to the window, picked up three plates heaped with food, scurried to a table with them and was back a moment later to fill glasses with soda. I bet she loved sitting down and taking her shoes off at the end of the day.

I munched on my sandwich and thought about Deirdre at the bank. The general consensus around town was that Mr. Goran had burned down his barn for the insurance money. Only one person besides Aram and me had sent Mr. Goran flowers. That person was a loan officer at the bank. I couldn't help wondering why.

The tellers' counter was up front. In the back was a warren of cubicles where I immediately spotted a familiar face—Donald Curtis, the realtor. He came out of a cubicle, shook a man's hand and walked past me. Either he didn't notice me or he didn't recognize me. I headed for the cubicles. That had to be where the loan officers worked. But I was stopped by a woman with a bank-security pass hanging from a chain around her neck.

"Can I help you?"

"I'm here to see Deirdre," I said.

The woman eyed me skeptically. "Deirdre Parker? Do you have an appointment?"

"No, but—"

"Deirdre isn't in today."

"Do you know how I could reach her?"

The woman's eyes narrowed. "For bank business, you can reach her here."

In other words, she wasn't going to tell me. I would simply have to come back again.

THIRTEEN

I arrived home just as Aunt Ginny was getting into her car to go to work.

"Don't use the washing machine," she said. "There's a leak somewhere."

I knew that already. I was the one who had told her.

"I put in a service call. Someone's coming to look at it. I left a key."

"Will you be home tonight?" I asked.

"If I am, it'll be late. Don't wait up for me."

I was definitely rooting for her being late. It would make things easier for me.

I made something to eat. I watched TV. I checked online for directions to the go-kart park and decided when I should leave.

My phone pinged. A text from IT.

Retrieved info from drive. Will clean up & email prob tmrrw.

I replied with thanks. Ten minutes before I was ready to go, my cell phone rang. This time it was Ashleigh.

"Do you want to find out what Maddy called Mike about?" she asked breathlessly.

"Where are you?"

"At the end of your driveway. Grab your bike. Let's go. You don't want to miss them."

I grabbed my bicycle lights and ran outside. Ashleigh was waiting for me at the end of the driveway. We rode single file, Ashleigh in the lead, up the road and away from town. It was a hot, sticky summer night. Ashleigh set the pace. It wasn't long before my T-shirt was soaked through.

Ashleigh raised her hand to signal a stop. She dismounted and switched off her lights. I did the same.

"It's over there." She pointed to bright lights in the distance. "We'll leave our bikes here and go in the back way, where the snack bar is."

We stashed our bikes in the bushes. Ashleigh detached one of her bike lights and focused it on the ground.

"Stick close," she said.

We made our way slowly along a partly over-grown path through scrub and brush. Twice I tripped on roots sticking out of the ground. Once I fell and skinned my knee. We kept going until Ashleigh held up her hand again.

"There it is." She pointed at a rectangular struc-ture looming ahead of us. Light shone through its windows. "That's the kitchen. Mike always brings out the garbage at the end of his shift."

I stared at her. "How do you know that?"

"Taylor and I have been out here with Maddy before. She always wants someone to go with her for moral support." She broke off, grabbed my arm and yanked me down to the ground, a finger pressed to her lips to signal me to keep me quiet. "Maddy's here," she hissed.

I started to raise my head for a look, but Ashleigh held me down.

We crouched in the bush. Light suddenly flooded the area behind the snack bar. A door clattered shut.

"What's so important?" a voice said. Mike.

"Jonathan told me that girl asked you where you were the night of the fire. He said she accused you of starting the fire and that the cops were going to question you." That was Maddy.

"Yeah? So?"

"So I wanted to tell you that you don't have anything to worry about. I said you were with me."

"You talked to the cops about me?"

"Not the cops. The girl. Riley. She asked about you, and I told her we were together and there was no way you had anything to do with the fire."

"Why'd you do that?" Mike sounded far from relieved, never mind grateful.

"Because I don't want you to get into trouble."

"This is none of your business. Jeez, Maddy, why did you have to go and complicate things?"

"Complicate things?" She sounded stunned. "I was just trying to help."

"I don't need help."

"But Mike—"

"I don't need help, I don't need your alibi, and I sure don't need you messing around in stuff that has nothing to do with you. And where's my jacket? I'm tired of asking you for it."

"It's in my locker at work."

"I want it back."

"But you gave it to me."

"I *loaned* it to you one night when you were whining about being cold. It's my football jacket. I want it back."

"But I thought we were—"

"You thought we were what? We're friends, that's all. But we're not going to stay friends if I have to keep asking you for my stuff."

"We're more than friends," Maddy said. "Remember when we—"

"Friends. Period."

"Come on, Mike. After everything I've done for you—"

"What? What have you done for me except stick your big nose into my business? Stay out of it. I mean it."

"But Mike—"

There was another flood of light. Someone must have opened the door to the snack bar.

"Wait, Mike—"

"Leave me alone. Just leave me alone, okay?"

The light dwindled to a sliver and then vanished altogether. I heard the click of a lock. Then silence, followed by sniffling. Maddy was crying. The sound faded along with her footsteps. Ashleigh led the way back to our bikes.

"What do you think that was all about?" she asked when we got there.

I'd been thinking about it the whole way back. "I'm not sure. You?"

"It sounds to me like Maddy was lying when she told us she was with Mike the night of the fire."

"It does, doesn't it?"

"Why do you think Mike didn't want her to alibi him?" Ashleigh asked. "You think it's because he had nothing to do with the fire? Or do you think there's another reason?"

"I don't know." A person doesn't need an alibi if he hasn't done anything wrong. "Maybe he already has an alibi. He told me he was with friends."

"Like Maddy."

"He didn't say Maddy. He didn't say friend. He said friends, with an *s*."

We switched on our bike lights.

"Mike said Madison had complicated things for him," Ashleigh said slowly. "What do you think he meant by that?"

"I don't know." But I was thinking about it. Had she ruined Mike's plans for setting up an alibi? He'd told me he was with friends. Had some of them agreed to cover for him? Or was there something else going on?

"Maybe he really didn't do it," Ashleigh said.

Or maybe he didn't do it alone, I thought. What if Mike and his father had set the fire together? What if they'd been planning to alibi each other if they had to? Or what if Ted was the arsonist, and Mike planned to alibi him if it came to that?

Except Ted had already told the other volunteer firefighters that he was at the cemetery that night because it was his father's birthday. And Mike had given me his alibi.

Maybe Ashleigh was right, and all Mike meant was that if Madison lied for him and the police found out, it would make him look guilty of something. On the other hand, it could mean that he was guilty but was afraid Madison's lies would point the police in his direction. There were so many possibilities, and all I could say was, "I can't tell from what they said if Mike was involved or not."

It was well past midnight by the time we got to my house, so I asked Ashleigh to stay over rather than ride all the way back into town in the dark. She agreed and texted her parents, and we went up to my room to settle in. It wasn't long before I heard Ashleigh's breathing slow down. I lay awake on the other side of the bed and stared at the ceiling.

Madison had said she wanted to help Mike.

Mike told her he didn't need an alibi.

What did that mean?

Ashleigh woke me the next morning instead of the other way around. She had to get to work.

"I'll text you," she said before she rode off.

Aunt Ginny got home a few minutes later and went straight to bed. I logged in to my email to see if IT had sent me anything from Aram's hard drive.

He had. He'd sent me a lot. I scanned through the file names and clicked on one of the photos to make sure they were retrievable. They were. They were all pictures of the farm next door. Mr. Goran's farm. He must have sent them to Aram, and he must have done it in the past year and a half or so, because before that he didn't live here. If that was true, then it was also true that Aram *had* heard from his father, despite what he'd told Aunt Ginny and me.

Curious, I clicked on a file called *Farm Finances.* It contained records from the farm—what was planted, projected yield, actual yield, plans for the coming years, expenses and revenues. Why did Aram have this information? I decided to check the file of email that IT had recovered. That's when I figured out that it wasn't Aram's computer at all.

I ran into Aunt Ginny's room and shook her awake.

Without even opening her eyes, she said, "Go away, Riley."

"I need to ask you something."

"Not now." She rolled over.

I shook her again. "It's important."

She opened one eye. It shot daggers at me. "It had better be. I haven't had a decent night's sleep since we moved in."

"I need to speak to Aram."

Both eyes opened and immediately narrowed. "What for?"

"I have to ask him something."

"Details."

"Please, Aunt Ginny, I need to talk to him for just a minute, but I can't tell you what it's about. Not yet." I don't like thinking the best of people and finding out the worst. I especially don't like being lied to. It makes me angry. If I told Aunt Ginny what I'd found, the chances were excellent that I would never be able to speak to Aram. I didn't want that. I wanted to look him in the eye and ask him two questions. I wanted to see his face when he answered.

But Aunt Ginny said, "I don't want you going over there, Riley."

"*Going over there*? You mean he's at home? I thought you arrested him."

"He got lucky at the bail hearing, because of his father being in the hospital. The judge made him surrender his passport. He's not allowed to leave the county without notifying the court. But you're not to go over there, do you understand?"

I made a tactical surrender and said I understood perfectly. I left her and waited thirty minutes, until I heard her snoring through her solid-oak bedroom door. I tiptoed downstairs and took the short way across the yard to Mr. Goran's farm.

Aram answered the door on the second ring. He looked tired but otherwise the same.

"I'm surprised that aunt of yours let you come over here," he said.

"I need to ask you something."

"Come in."

"Right here is fine. You lied about that computer."

"Is that your question?" He ran his fingers through his already disheveled hair. "I assume your friend was able to retrieve some information from the hard drive."

"He was. Enough to prove that you lied to Aunt Ginny when you said the computer was yours."

"I see." He didn't argue with me or protest that the computer really was his. "And you're wondering why I said that."

"It's called tampering with evidence." Or something like that. I was pretty sure it was against the law. I was positive that Aunt Ginny would be outraged if she knew he'd misled her about who owned the computer found in Mr. Goran's house and how it had gotten smashed.

"Does your aunt know?" Aram asked.

I wasn't about to answer that question, not when I still had a few of my own.

"Did you try to wreck your father's computer?"

"No. It was broken when I got here. And if anything, I was trying to protect my father until I knew more about what had happened."

"How do I know you're telling the truth? How do I know you weren't the one who tried to destroy it?"

"Why would I do that?" He seemed genuinely perplexed.

"So that nobody would find anything incriminating on it."

"Riley, what are you talking about?"

"You told me you hadn't been in contact with your father in years. Was that a lie too?"

"No."

I tried to read his face, searching for any clue to what he was thinking. I found nothing.

"Then why is there an email from you on your father's hard drive?"

"I don't know what you're talking about. I never emailed him."

A car turned in to the driveway and raced toward us, traveling faster than seemed wise and shooting gravel all over the place. It was Aunt Ginny. She came to a stop, got out of the car and shouted, "What part of *no* don't you understand, Riley? Get over here and into the car this minute. I mean it."

I looked at Aram. "I read the email, Aram."

"I didn't send any email."

I couldn't tell what he was thinking. "Are you lying to me again?"

"No." He met my eyes. "I'm not."

"Riley, did you hear me? Get over here. *Now!*"

I had no choice. I waved the white flag again, and again it was a tactical maneuver. So was the apologizing I did all the way down Mr. Goran's driveway and all the way up ours.

"I just wanted to see that he was okay."

"I said no."

"But he's a neighbor."

"Damn it, Riley, I said no. And when I say no, I expect you to obey, especially when it comes to police matters."

"But—"

She gave me the fiercest look I had ever seen. She definitely needed more sleep, but she wasn't going to get it if she kept yelling at me.

"Sorry, Aunt Ginny." If you ask me, I sounded genuinely contrite. I weighed the pros and cons of telling her what had made it so important that I talk to Aram. She was already furious with me. If she found out I had taken Mr. Goran's computer, she would be enraged, possibly even homicidal. Of course, I hadn't known it belonged to Mr. Goran when I took the hard drive. I thought it was Aram's. But I doubted Aunt Ginny would be able, let alone willing, to make the distinction. She would throw it all onto the ever-growing heap of What Happens When Riley Meddles, and she would punish me accordingly. Unless, of course, I could get to the bottom of this new development myself, in which case she would still become enraged but would be forced to concede, given the outcome, that punishment was perhaps not warranted.

Someone had sent Mr. Goran that email. It said it was from Aram. It was possible it wasn't. Either way, that email had set the stage for everything that followed.

FOURTEEN

"I'm sorry." Two words that people don't hear often enough, according to Jimmy. Two words that go a long way toward placating the aggrieved party. Two words you'd think were made out of gold, so reluctant are some people to part with them. Two words that, once spoken, usually bring peace. The lesson Jimmy meant to impart was, if you're in the wrong, apologize. There is an equally valid lesson, deduced from living with Aunt Ginny. If someone *thinks* you're in the wrong and is therefore angry with you, apologize.

"I really am, Aunt Ginny," I said. "I know you want me to do the right thing, not just whatever pops into my head. And I didn't do that. And I'm sorry."

"Well, I should hope so," she grumbled. There wasn't anything more to say that I hadn't said already. Apologizing always worked with Aunt Ginny. She went back to bed, and I went into town.

I was locking my bike to a No Parking sign near one of the town's two funeral homes when Mike and his buddies sauntered out of a store right in front of me. Mike scowled when he saw me but started to circle around me.

"How's your dad?" I asked.

Mike turned. "As if you care."

"I do." I cared because I didn't want anything bad to happen to Aram. But I also cared because, well, why wouldn't I? Ted Winters hadn't exactly made a good impression on me, but that didn't mean I wanted him to be hurt or worse.

"You're a friend of the guy who put my dad in the hospital. And of the old man too. You don't care about my dad or my grandfather. He died—did you know that?"

I nodded. Mike's friends had gathered around.

"He died because he was expecting to get his farm back and he didn't. It wasn't fair. My grandfather made that place what it is, and this guy who wasn't even born here comes and steals it from him. And because of that, my grandfather died."

Behind him, Mike's friends nodded.

"I'm sorry your grandfather lost his farm, Mike," I said. "And I'm sorry he died. But that's no reason—"

He stepped toward me.

I stood my ground.

"I'm sorry about your dad too," I said. "But that fire in Mr. Goran's barn was set on purpose, and Mr. Goran was locked inside. If the fire department hadn't arrived when it did, he would be dead now. Maybe that's what the arsonist intended."

"I had nothing to do with it," Mike said. "Neither did my dad. And if that old man doesn't make it, I'm not going to be sorry."

"What do you have against him? You don't even know him," I said.

"I don't want to know him. I don't want anything to do with him."

"Then why did you keep breaking into his barn?" I asked.

"He had something that belonged to me. He wouldn't give it back."

"You mean the horse brasses?"

Mike seemed surprised that I knew about them. "My grandpa meant for me to have them."

"Maybe if you'd been nicer, Mr. Goran would have given them to you. But you weren't. You trashed him every chance you got. You trespassed on his property. You wouldn't let your friends accept that donation from him. Then you sent him that phony email—"

"What email? What donation? What are you talking about?"

"You know what email. You sent it."

"You're crazy."

"Were you hoping he'd sell the farm? Is that it, Mike? Were you hoping he'd sell it cheap enough that your dad would be able to get his hands on it? Was that the idea?"

Mike stepped so close to me that I could smell bacon on his breath. His hands clenched into fists. One of Mike's friends—one of the smarter ones—touched him on the arm.

"We should go," he said. "Your mom has enough to worry about without having to bail you out of jail. Her aunt's a cop, remember?"

Mike didn't retreat, but he didn't come at me either. His friend tugged on his arm. Mike finally let himself be led away. The rest of his buddies trailed after him. I watched them go. When I turned again, Charlie was coming up the street, a bulging plastic supermarket bag hanging from each hand.

"Was that Mike?" he asked.

I nodded. "You need help?"

In answer, he handed me one of the bags. It was heavy.

"Pineapple, half a dozen oranges and two melons," Charlie said. "If you had them in a box and were carrying them close to your chest, it would be no big deal. But with all that weight concentrated in one place and hanging from one small piece of plastic, it feels like it weighs a ton."

He was right about that. A few moments later we turned the corner and he led me up a walkway to an old-fashioned brick house with a wraparound verandah and white trim. It looked like something out of a storybook.

"This is your house?" I asked.

"Yeah. I could use something cold to drink. You?"

He led me around back, and we clattered through a wood-framed screen door into a huge, spotless kitchen. The whole place smelled like cinnamon.

"My mom was baking for the church," Charlie said. He opened the fridge and grabbed a couple of cans of soda. He tossed one to me. "What did Mike want?" A glance at me led him to amend his question. "What did you want with Mike?" He flipped open the tab on his can, took a long swallow and sank down onto one of the kitchen chairs. I told him what I'd found on my computer and what I suspected.

"What did this email say?" Charlie asked.

"It's supposedly from Aram."

"Supposedly?"

"Aram says he didn't send it."

Charlie seemed to be struggling to understand what I was saying. "Okay. So how do you get from there to thinking Mike sent it?"

"The email says that an extremist group is making him write the email and that he's being held hostage."

"That must be an old email. Aram told us he was held hostage a few years ago."

"It isn't. It's recent. It was sent just a couple of days before the fire. Think about it, Charlie. You want to get Mr. Goran's farm away from him. You know he has a son. So you send a fake email to Mr. Goran saying his son has been kidnapped and that if Mr. Goran doesn't raise the ransom money, his son will be killed. What if whoever sent that email did it because they wanted him to sell the farm to raise the ransom money? But…" It was falling into place now. "Say he went to the bank and arranged a loan." I told him about Deirdre Parker and the bamboo plant she had delivered to the hospital. "It's the only way she could know Mr. Goran. She arranged a loan for him so he didn't have to sell the farm. So then the only way Mike could get even with him was to set his barn on fire."

"There's just one thing," Charlie said.

"What?"

"I don't think Mike is smart enough to pull off something like that. He's not even smart enough to think of something like that."

"It's not exactly the most brilliant idea in the world."

"Yeah, but it means Mike had to know that Mr. Goran had a son, what his son's name was and where he worked. And this is a guy who couldn't find Afghanistan on a map if his life depended on it. He probably can't even spell Afghanistan. He got fifty percent in world geography, Riley, and it was a pity pass. Mr. Randall didn't want him back in his class again. Ever."

"So maybe it wasn't Mike. Maybe it was his dad. He would have known how to find out about Aram."

"I don't know." Charlie still sounded doubtful. "I know Mike pretty well. His dad too—at least, his reputation. I've never heard anyone say anything bad about him. The opposite, in fact. He's well liked, Riley. Well regarded too. How well do you know Aram?"

He had a point. I at least had a good reason, Aunt Ginny notwithstanding, to believe that Mr. Goran had not started that fire. But what did I know about Aram, other than that he was a sort of prodigal son? He had lied to the police—Aunt Ginny—about the computer. So why was I so eager to believe he was telling the truth about that email?

"You're right," I said. "Do you have a computer?"

Charlie rolled his eyes. "Do I have a computer? It's a small town, Riley, not a technological wasteland."

He led me up to his room, where he had a laptop, a tablet and an iPhone.

"Take your pick."

I chose the laptop, went online, got into my email account and shot off an email to IT. He responded immediately, and I had to pull up the attachment with Mr. Goran's email file in it to give him what he wanted.

"I still don't get it," Charlie said. "It's not like Ted could give the farm back to his father the way he originally planned."

"Maybe he wanted to pass it on to Mike."

"I don't think Mike wants to be a farmer."

I was starting to get impatient. "Okay, so maybe he just wanted to force Mr. Goran out. I know Mike did. He also wanted his horse brasses. That's why he kept breaking into the barn. It's also why he stopped your team from taking that donation—he hated Mr. Goran and didn't want anyone else to like him."

"My team?" Charlie looked baffled. "Oh. That wasn't—"

My cell phone pinged. It was Ashleigh: **On break. Mike news?**

While I texted her back, Charlie turned the computer around so that he could read the email signed by Aram.

Ashleigh was working a long shift and then had to go straight home. Her grandma was visiting.

We agreed to meet up the next day. I slipped my phone back into my pocket. Charlie was still reading what was on the screen, except now it wasn't the same email.

"You said you thought that whoever sent that email to Mr. Goran wanted to force him to sell his farm, right?" he asked, frowning.

"Right."

"And that he must have got a loan from the bank so he didn't have to sell."

"Or something like that," I said. Unless, of course, Aram really had sent that email and had been trying to get money from his estranged father. Was that also the reason he'd showed up here? To profit from the sale of the farm should his father die? I heard Aunt Ginny's voice in my ear. *Just because someone tells you something doesn't make it so.* "Assuming that Ted and Mike were behind the fire."

"Which assumes that Mr. Goran got the loan he needed from the bank. But he didn't." He turned the laptop around so that I could see the screen. "Read this."

This was a letter on bank letterhead, turning down a loan application made by Mr. Goran. The letter was dated the day before the fire. I stared at it, stunned.

"You know what that means, right, Riley?"

I did. But I didn't want to admit it.

"*If* Mr. Goran believed his son was kidnapped," Charlie said, "and *if* he thought he needed money for a ransom, and—this is the big one, Riley—*if* the bank turned him down, then he could have decided to commit insurance fraud to get the money. That would raise the ransom he needed but save him from having to sell the farm."

I stared at Charlie. He was saying out loud exactly what I was thinking: "He might be guilty, just like everyone says he is."

I stared at the letter. There was one thing Charlie hadn't said. That if he was right about what he had just laid out, then it was also possible that Aram had sent the email that started everything. Aram had pushed his father to arson.

As I walked back to my bike, I made a phone call. Twenty minutes later I stepped into the bank and announced to the woman at the information desk that I had an appointment with Deirdre Parker.

"Riley Donovan," I said in answer to Deirdre's puzzled look. "I just called you about an appointment."

"You're much younger than I expected," she said. "What can I do for you? Not a loan, surely."

"Well, sort of," I said.

Her puzzlement deepened. "Please, sit down. Are you a young entrepreneur? An Internet whiz, perhaps?"

"It's about Mr. Goran," I said.

Her body tensed. "I'm not sure I can—"

"He applied for a loan here," I said.

"Even if that were true," she said, "I certainly can't discuss it with you. Our privacy policies—"

"I know it's true. I have a copy of the email you sent him, turning down his application. It was on his computer hard drive, and now it's on mine." Not to mention on my ISP's server and probably still on IT's computer. "Did he tell you why he wanted the money?"

"I can't discuss that with you."

"Is that why you left that plant for him at the hospital? Did you feel bad about turning him down?"

Her face was crimson. She stood up abruptly.

"Now see here—" she began angrily.

"Is there a problem, Deirdre?"

We both turned to look at the man who had spoken.

"No, Mr. Kincaid," Deirdre said. "No problem. This young lady just wants some information, and I'm doing my best to help her."

"Well, as long as you don't keep any real customers waiting."

"I won't, Mr. Kincaid."

He was the same man I'd seen shaking hands with Donald Curtis the last time I was in the bank. He gave me a stern look before moving on. Through the glass, I saw him head for the bank's main door.

I turned back to Deirdre Parker.

"About Mr. Goran," I said.

"I'm afraid I can't help you."

"He didn't need a loan to keep his farm going," I said. "He needed it for something else. But you turned him down. I was just wondering why. He has a valuable piece of property, and you could always sell it if he wasn't able to make the payments."

"The bank is not in the real-estate business. And any decisions we make about a client are confidential, which means I can't discuss them with anyone." She stood up. "I have to ask you to leave. You're putting me in an awkward position."

I remembered what Sharon and Carol had said. "I know you need this job. I know you're a single mother. And I know you feel bad about turning Mr. Goran down. No one else sent him an expensive plant. Just you."

To my astonishment, she sat down and started to cry.

"Please don't ask me any more questions about this. Don't tell anyone anything. If Mr. Kincaid found out, he'd fire me for sure."

"If he found out what?"

She stood up again.

"You have to go." Her face had hardened. "If you don't, I'll have security escort you to the door."

She wasn't going to tell me anything else. She was clearly nervous. She jumped when her phone rang. "Mr. Kincaid." She looked rattled.

There was nothing else I could do. I left.

I walked back to my bike. I knew now that Mr. Goran had applied for a bank loan and that Deirdre Parker had turned him down. Was that why she had sent him

that plant? Did she think she had driven him to arson?
Or was there more? She had seemed so shaken by my
questions. Had she been enlisted by Ted Winters to try
to force Mr. Goran to sell his farm? Was she nervous
because I had proof of her involvement that I might
show her boss, Mr. Kincaid, not to mention the police?
Or was there something else going on?

No matter what her role had been or why she had
denied his loan, it didn't make Mr. Goran *look* any
better. In fact, to a lot of people it would make him
look worse. If people knew about the loan, it would
only solidify their conviction that he had burned
down his barn to collect the insurance money.

There was a pickup truck in the driveway when I got
home. I figured it was probably the washing-machine
repairman Aunt Ginny had finally hired.

My cell phone pinged again. A text from IT. **Check
your email.**

I dropped my bike at the bottom of the porch
steps and raced up to my room.

FIFTEEN

Halfway up the stairs, I heard something. Probably the repairman.

"I'll be down in a minute," I called.

Silence. *Whatever.*

I continued up the stairs.

I walked down the hall to my room.

As soon as I crossed the threshold, I got a weird feeling, as if the hair on the back of my neck was standing up. But everything looked exactly as I had left it. I sat down at my desk and turned on my computer. A moment later I was in my email and reading with amazement what IT had been able to find out.

Things happened fast after that.

I heard another sound. Thumping.

I started to turn.

Something was pulled over my head. A sack or a pillowcase. I couldn't see.

Someone grabbed me from behind and lifted me off my chair. I was half-carried and half-dragged across the room and thrown like a sack of dirty laundry into my closet.

The door slammed shut and something scraped across the floor.

Something heavy.

My trunk.

Even the movers had complained when they had to carry it upstairs, and they were big guys.

I waited a few seconds to make sure that whoever had pushed me in there wasn't still standing outside, and then I threw myself against the door. It didn't move. Not right away. I pushed and kicked and pushed some more, moving it inch by inch.

Footsteps thundered down the stairs.

I pushed again and made just enough room to squeeze through.

My computer was gone.

I didn't stop to think. I raced after the intruder. I was hoping it was Mike. I was afraid it might be Aram.

I reached the top of the stairs and heard the intruder in the kitchen below. I yelled for him to stop. Don't ask me why. It wasn't like he was going to obey.

I took the stairs two at a time, clinging to the banister to keep from falling.

I heard a crash.

I ran through the kitchen to the back door.

The intruder was sprawled facedown on the gravel. He'd tripped over my bicycle, at the bottom of the steps. My computer lay on the ground a few feet from him. There was no way to tell if it was okay.

The intruder, who was definitely not Mike or Aram, groaned, untangled himself and sat up. He had a gun in his hand. It was pointed at me.

I started to back away.

The intruder cursed as he got to his feet. His knee buckled, and he let out another groan. In that nano-second, while he was distracted, I ran back into the house and slammed the kitchen door. I tried to lock it, but he was already forcing it open, and he was much stronger than I was. I ran for the stairs.

I heard his uneven footfalls behind me.

I raced into Aunt Ginny's room, dove into her closet and dug my cell phone out of my pocket.

A floorboard creaked nearby. He was in the bedroom. I held my breath.

I heard another sound downstairs.

"Riley?" Aunt Ginny was home. "Riley, for Pete's sake, do you have to leave your bike right in the way?" Silence. Then her voice again, more impatient now. "I know you're here. Riley. Answer me."

I didn't dare.

I heard footsteps again, running this time but still uneven. A voice barked, "Freeze!" and then, "Drop it."

Something clattered to the floor.

I snuck out of the closet and into the hallway. The intruder was standing halfway down the stairs, with his hands in the air. Aunt Ginny was at the bottom, her gun trained on him. Her eyes flicked to me, but only for a second.

"Are you okay?"

"Yes." Other than shaking all over, I was fine.

"Call 9-1-1. Tell them there's an intruder."

I did as she said. Aunt Ginny ordered the intruder to make his way slowly down the stairs and lie face-down on the floor.

He complied.

"He tried to steal my computer," I told Aunt Ginny. "He locked me in my closet."

She kept her gun trained on him.

"What else did you take?" she demanded.

"I want a lawyer," he said.

"He works with Donald Curtis," I said.

"Who?"

I told her about my encounter with Curtis at Mr. Goran's farm. "He was asking about buying the place."

"Don't say anything else, Riley," Aunt Ginny said. "We're going to wait for backup, and then I'm going to charge him with break-and-enter, assault and forcible confinement. That ought to put him out of action for a few years."

"Now wait a minute," the man said, looking alarmed. "I never hurt her."

Aunt Ginny didn't respond. She held her weapon steady on him and demanded his name.

"Johnston. Tom Johnston. I've lived in this town all my life. Used to have a job at the feed store before it closed down. Now folks have to drive close to two hours to get their feed."

Aunt Ginny was not moved.

"I got kids," Johnston said. "I want them to have a future."

"What they're going to have is a father in jail," Aunt Ginny said.

"How about a deal? How about I tell you who sent me here?"

"You'll have to do better than that," Aunt Ginny said. "You broke into my house."

He blanched "*your* house?" I don't think he'd realized until then that he had burglarized a police officer's house.

"You have a weapon. You threatened my niece with it."

"It's not even loaded," he whimpered. "I didn't want the darned thing, but he insisted, said I might have to throw a scare into someone."

"He? Who's he?" Aunt Ginny demanded.

"Curtis."

Aunt Ginny glanced at me.

"Did he pay you to break into Mr. Goran's house too?" I asked.

"Riley!" Aunt Ginny shot me a warning glance. But she couldn't help herself. "Did he?" she asked.

"He said there was no one there. But someone pulled up not long after I got inside. As soon as I heard that, I ran. No one was hurt."

"What were you supposed to do in Mr. Goran's house?"

"Just take the computer, that's all."

"What computer?" Aunt Ginny asked.

"Mr. Goran didn't have a computer."

"Yes, he did," I said. "But Mr. Johnston didn't take it. Did you?"

"I got scared when I heard someone coming. I dropped it. Then I stomped on it."

"Why did Curtis want the computer?"

"I don't know. He didn't tell me. I swear. He said to make it look like kids had broken in, trashed the place and stolen the computer."

"The letter," I said. I remembered Deirdre Parker's phone call from Mr. Kincaid as I was leaving. Had she told him I had a copy of her letter on my hard drive? "Is that why you broke in here? To steal my computer?"

"Your computer? What would anyone want with your computer?" Aunt Ginny asked. "And what letter are you talking about?"

"It's a long story, Aunt Ginny. And I think"—actually, I was positive—"that it has something to do with the fire. I think Mr. Curtis and maybe Mr. Kincaid know something about it."

For sure Deirdre Parker was involved too, but I didn't want to mention her name yet, not if I didn't have to.

"Kincaid?"

"The bank manager. Both the email with the bank letter and the email from an extremist group came from the same server. The bank's secure server."

"Extremist group? I don't care how long your story is, you'd better start talking, young lady," Aunt Ginny said.

"I think Mr. Kincaid and Mr. Curtis tried to trick Mr. Goran into thinking he needed money to pay a ransom to an extremist group if he wanted Aram to be released. They made sure he couldn't get that money from the bank. I have proof. They wanted to force him to sell the farm."

"But instead Mr. Goran found another way to get the money he needed," Aunt Ginny mused.

"Maybe not," I said. "Maybe they paid Mr. Johnston here to set fire to the barn to make Mr. Goran look bad. Maybe they even told him to lock Mr. Goran inside."

"Now you just wait a minute," Johnston said. "I had nothing to do with that barn fire. I swear it. I wasn't anywhere near the place that night, and I can prove it."

"What about Curtis?" Aunt Ginny asked.

"I can't say he was unhappy when he heard about the fire. Said it would make things easier all around."

"I don't believe you," I said.

"I'm telling you the truth. Curtis wanted the place, all right. He has big plans for the land," Johnston said. "He said he had a partner who was going to help him."

"Who is this partner?" Aunt Ginny asked.

I was pretty sure I already knew—Mr. Kincaid.

"He didn't tell me. He just said she could make sure the seller was motivated."

She?

"By making Mr. Goran think he needed money and then denying him a loan. Have I got that right?" Aunt Ginny asked.

I'd been wrong about Deirdre Parker. I'd told her what I had on my hard drive. She must have told

Curtis, who dispatched Johnston to dispose of the problem. I guess he'd never heard of backups. But why had Deirdre gone along with the plan? The plant she'd sent to Mr. Goran seemed to suggest she was sorry for what had happened. Or maybe she'd just wanted to give that impression.

"Nobody mentioned anything about a fire, and I swear on my mother's grave, I never set one. I broke into the old man's house. Your place too. But I never hurt anyone. I told you everything I know, and you have to believe me when I tell you I would never set a fire deliberately."

"What about Ted Winters?" I asked. "Do you know who beat him up?"

"Riley, please—" Aunt Ginny began.

"No," Johnston said. "Curtis asked me to rough him up some. He wanted to get Goran's son out of the way. The idea was, I'd say I'd seen Aram fleeing the scene. But I told Curtis the same thing I told you. I don't hurt people, especially good people like Ted."

"Do you know who did?"

"No. I swear."

Tires crunched on the gravel outside. Car doors slammed. Aunt Ginny shouted, and Josh Martin appeared, along with two uniformed cops. Aunt Ginny directed the uniforms to handcuff Mr. Johnston while she explained to Josh what had just happened.

He frowned. "Computer? What computer? What are you talking about?"

Aunt Ginny filled him in. "I'm surprised you didn't seize the computer as part of your arson investigation," she added. The remark sounded innocent enough, but the look in her eyes was pure wolf. She had caught Josh in a rookie error, and she wasn't about to let it slide by unnoticed.

Josh called out to one of the uniforms. "I thought I told you to find anything relevant in the old man's house."

"I did," the officer said, apparently confused by what was going on.

"He had a computer. How come I never saw it?"

"That old man had a computer?" The officer shook his head. "I never saw it."

"Did you look?" Josh was barely managing to keep his anger in check.

"Well, no. I mean, who would have figured—?"

Josh dismissed him with the wave of a hand and ordered him to take the prisoner in. He turned back to me. "Do you think your computer still works?"

It did. I showed him and Aunt Ginny the email and the letter from Deirdre, turning down Mr. Goran's loan application. I also told them my suspicions.

I made a formal statement at the police station. While I waited for Aunt Ginny, two uniformed officers brought in Donald Curtis. He was full of bluster, angrily demanding to know why he was being brought in for questioning like a common criminal. His bluster evaporated when Aunt Ginny paraded Tom Johnston past him. Then she made him sweat it out a little longer while she brought Deirdre Parker in for questioning—and made sure that Curtis saw her too. Aunt Ginny told me that Deirdre confessed everything.

"She'd been doing some freelance secretarial work for Curtis to make some extra money," Aunt Ginny said. "Once, against her better instincts she says, she accepted money in return for giving him some information about a bank customer. If anyone had found out, she would have been fired immediately. Curtis used that to blackmail her into helping him get his hands on Mr. Goran's farm."

Confronted with Deirdre's statement, Curtis admitted to his part in the scheme. He seemed to think no great harm had been done. His plan hadn't worked, after all.

"What about the fire? It put Mr. Goran in the hospital," I said.

"He insists he didn't have anything to do with the fire," Aunt Ginny said.

"And you believe him?"

"He says once the fire happened, he figured the farm would be his for sure. And then Aram showed up, and he was in no rush to sell off his father's place. So Curtis exploited Ted Winters's animosity toward Aram's father and then toward Aram. He heard about what happened at the market and then about their altercation in front of the café. He admits to assaulting Ted. His plan was to jump him from behind and claim he saw Aram. But Ted must have heard him, because he started to turn around just as Curtis was about to clobber him, and the next thing Curtis knew, he was in what he called 'a fight for his life.' He claims that what happened to Ted was in self-defense." She shook her head at the logic. "The grand plan was to get Aram arrested and out of the way."

"And Ted couldn't tell that it wasn't Aram?"

"Curtis was wearing a balaclava."

"But Mrs. Winters said she recognized Aram…"

Aunt Ginny just shook her head. "Eyewitness testimony can be shaky at best. But on a dark night, after already seeing Aram and her husband together, she could have thought that's what she saw."

"Or she could have been lying."

"It's possible," Aunt Ginny said. She didn't seem troubled by it. But, like I already said, she is suspicious by nature. It's an asset in her job.

"What are you going to do now?" I asked.

She lifted a thick file folder off her desk. I read the label.

"That's the arson report," I said.

"You were right about Aram," Aunt Ginny said. "I'm not discounting that you may be right about his father too. But somebody set that fire. I need to know everything there is to know about it."

The file was on the coffee table the next morning when I got up. Aunt Ginny was asleep on the couch. I tiptoed to the table, grabbed the file and read it while I ate breakfast.

"And what do you think you're doing?" Aunt Ginny, bleary-eyed, was in the doorway.

I flipped the file closed. "Nothing."

"You're snooping again." She glanced at the coffee-maker. It was empty.

"I'll make it." I put my cereal bowl in the sink and got the coffee out of the fridge. "There's a lot of information in there," I said. "Like this." I pointed. "It talks about burn rates and melt rates, how hot the fire was in certain places, how fast it burned, what damage was done."

"And?" Aunt Ginny had gotten herself a coffee mug and was eyeing the machine as it started to drip.

"What happened to the brasses?"

"Brasses?"

"Horse brasses." I explained how Mr. Goran had acquired them. "But there's no mention of them."

"Maybe he kept them somewhere else."

"He didn't. And when Aram did a walk-through of the damage, he found his father's keys. But no brasses."

"Maybe they melted," Aunt Ginny said.

"But the keys didn't."

"Maybe they have a different melting point."

"Could you find out, Aunt Ginny? Could you ask the fire marshal?"

She opened her mouth, I think to say no. But when I took her cup from her and filled it with coffee, she relented.

"I guess I could make a call," she said.

SIXTEEN

"What's the matter?" Ashleigh asked. "You haven't touched your ice cream. This is supposed to be a celebration."

"Yeah." Charlie frowned at me. "You got Aram out of jail. You figured out a ransom-blackmail scheme. You're a hero."

"But I still haven't cleared Mr. Goran. Curtis and Johnston deny having anything to do with the fire, and I have nothing that even begins to prove them wrong."

Ashleigh didn't say anything. Neither did Charlie. Instead, they exchanged glances.

"What?" I asked.

"Nothing," Ashleigh said.

"Yeah, nothing," Charlie agreed.

I studied their faces and shook my head. "You think Mr. Goran burned down his own barn, don't you?"

Ashleigh looked down at her sundae.

"Don't you, Ashleigh?" I said.

"If he did, would anyone really blame him?" Her eyes met mine. "He thought his son had been kidnapped. And Curtis made sure he couldn't take out a loan anywhere else. Maybe Mr. Goran thought he didn't have any choice."

"I bet if he gets a good lawyer, he can get off," Charlie added. "You know, considering that he was tricked."

"There's no way he would have set that fire or committed insurance fraud," I said.

"But he didn't actually commit fraud, did he?" Ashleigh said. "He didn't have a chance to contact the insurance company because he ended up in the hospital. So really, all he did was burn down his own property. Charlie's right. "I bet nothing happens to him." She paused. "Well, nothing legal, anyway."

I understood why they thought what they did— that Mr. Goran had started the fire. But I knew him better than they did, and not only was I positive that he would not do such a thing, I was equally sure he couldn't. Not with his past.

"Mike burned down that barn." It had to have been him. "Or his father did. Or both of them. I know it."

"I know you don't like Mike," Charlie said. "I'm not crazy about him either. But I don't think he did it."

"Or, at least, he didn't mean to lock Mr. Goran in," Ashleigh said.

"Are you serious?" Okay, so maybe I didn't understand why they thought what they did. "Look at the facts. Both Mike and his father hate Mr. Goran for buying the farm. They blame him for Clyde's death. Ted doesn't have a solid alibi for that night. He says he was visiting his father's grave, but he could be lying. No one saw him there. He could have set that fire. He could have locked Mr. Goran in the barn. Then, when he got the call about the fire and drove to the fire hall, he made sure that he mentioned that he'd been at the cemetery. When he finally got back to Mr. Goran's, he pretended he didn't hear Mr. Goran trying to get out of the barn."

"Maybe he really *didn't* hear him," Charlie said quietly.

I glowered at him.

"*And* Mike is lying about being with his friends. I know he is. He hates Mr. Goran as much as his father does. Maybe more. He broke into the barn more than once and bragged about it at school. You said so yourself, Ashleigh. He hassled Mr. Goran every chance he got. He trashed Aram's stall at the market. And, Charlie, he refused to allow your team to take that big donation from Mr. Goran, even though it meant you guys didn't win the prize."

Charlie went red in the face. "Riley—" he began.

Ashleigh cut him off. "What big donation?" she asked.

"The hundred-dollar donation that Charlie got from Mr. Goran."

"You got a hundred-dollar donation from Mr. Goran?" Ashleigh stared at him. "How come you never said anything about it to me?"

"Thanks a lot, Riley," Charlie muttered.

Uh-oh. I had promised not to tell.

"I'm sorry, Charlie."

He glowered across the table at me. "I would never tell anyone something you told me in confidence. I would never do that."

He stood up, dug some money out of his pocket and threw it onto the table before storming out of the café.

I don't know where Charlie went after he left the café, but it wasn't home. I learned that by camping out on his front steps for nearly an hour. He didn't answer my texts or calls. Finally, I decided to go looking for him. It only took forty-five minutes. Moorebridge isn't that big. I found him kicking around a soccer ball by himself in the park.

"Charlie?"

He spun around to face me.

"I really am sorry. If I could take it back, I would. Don't be mad at me."

He gave the soccer ball a halfhearted kick and watched it roll, slow down and finally settle a few yards away. He looked at it and then turned and looked at me.

"I'm mad at me, not you. I should have made them accept the donation. I should have said something when the money disappeared. But I didn't. I didn't do anything—except act like Mr. Goran was poison after that."

"I still shouldn't have said anything in front of Ashleigh," I said. "I promised not to."

Charlie shrugged as if he no longer cared. He started to fetch the ball. I followed—until something else caught my attention.

It was Mike. He was with Taylor, and they were walking toward the park's equipment shed. This was my chance. By the time I caught up with them, they were going into the staff locker room. The door was propped open with a bright-yellow trestle that sported the sign *Caution: Wet Floor*. I peeked inside. They were in front of Madison's locker.

"I don't know if this is such a good idea, Mike," Taylor was saying. I ducked back so I could listen without being seen.

"Come on, Taylor. Just do it, please. I've asked her a million times already."

"She says you gave it to her."

"She was whining about being cold. She asked me if she could borrow it. *Borrow*, Tay. I didn't give it to her. Think about it. Would I give my football jacket to *her*, of all people?"

I heard a sigh. "I guess not," Taylor said.

"She told me she had it at work. So go ahead. Open it."

"I don't know, Mike. I could get into big trouble if I get caught."

"Then you should get a move on."

Another sigh.

Footsteps.

I spun around.

It was Madison. She frowned when she saw me listening at the door and opened her mouth to say something—until she looked into the locker room to see what I was so interested in. She froze. Her mouth gaped.

"Hey, what are you doing?" she shouted.

Her locker was open, and Mike was reaching inside.

Madison flew at him and slammed the door shut.

"Hey!" Mike howled.

"That's private property. You have no right going in there." Madison glowered at Taylor. "You opened it, didn't you? You're the only person who has my combination—because you're *supposed* to be my friend."

"Mike asked me to get his jacket for him. He said you said it was okay." She turned to Mike as if daring him to deny it.

"I've asked you a million times, Maddy," Mike said. He didn't seem to care that Taylor's lie let her off the hook. "I want my jacket."

Madison stared at him in disbelief. Her lower lip trembled. "You gave it to me."

Mike shook his head impatiently. He elbowed Madison aside and opened the locker door.

From outside the clubhouse, Charlie's voice rang out. "Riley? Riley, are you in there?"

That's when Mike and Taylor turned and saw me for the first time. Mike looked like he wanted to spit on me. "What do *you* want?"

Since he was asking, I said, "You heard what happened, right, Mike?" They arrested someone for beating up your dad, and it wasn't Aram Goran. It was someone else. He confessed."

Mike said nothing.

"But the fire?" I said. "They still haven't arrested the person who did that."

"Yeah, but they know who it was. It was the old man." Mike was all snarl and sneer.

"But he didn't do it, did he, Mike?"

"Then who did?" Mike crossed his arms over his chest to wait for my answer.

"It was you," I said.

Mike laughed.

"You're crazy," Taylor said. "Why would Mike burn down his grandpa's barn?"

I ignored her.

"What's your alibi for that night, Mike?"

"Who do you think you are? The cops?" He started to turn back to Maddy.

"You told me you were with friends. Then Madison said you were with her. Which is it, Mike? Were you with Madison or with someone else?"

Mike spun around, his face beginning to flush, his eyes and nose squinched as if he were smelling something bad. "Look, I told you—I had nothing to do with that fire! Like Tay said, why would I burn down a barn my grandfather built?"

"Because you hated Mr. Goran. And because you wanted back what you thought he took from you."

"Those brasses are mine. He had no right to keep them."

"Funny thing about the brasses, Mike. They've disappeared."

"That old man probably took them out of the barn when he realized how valuable they are." He spit out the words like pieces of rancid meat. I had to hand it to him, he could really act. "What did he do? Sell them on eBay or something?"

"He didn't sell them. *You* took them, Mike. You took the brasses, and you started that fire. Maybe you even locked Mr. Goran in the barn."

"I didn't do anything!" He slammed the sole of his sneaker into the locker in front of him. The sound of impact reverberated in the metal-lined room.

"Those brasses were hanging in the barn the afternoon of the fire. I saw them myself," I said. "And now they're gone."

"*What*?" Mike's face drained of color. "What do you mean, *gone*?"

"Did they melt?" Taylor asked. She laid a hand on Mike's arm. "That's what probably happened. If they were in the barn during the fire, they would have melted."

"Did that stupid Paki let my brasses get burned up?" Mike balled his hands into fists. I thought he was going to punch out a locker, but he didn't, although he looked as though he might at any time.

His attitude perplexed me. Was he really that good an actor?

"They didn't melt," I said. "The fire wasn't hot enough. I checked with the fire marshal."

"So where are they? Who took them? What happened to them?" Again he seemed genuinely upset. Too genuine. Too upset. Did he think I was going to buy that?

"Drop the act, Mike," I said. "You were the one who wanted the brasses. You were the one who broke into the barn. You're the one who trashed the table at the market. You're the one who tried to turn your team at school against Mr. Goran's donation, and when that didn't work, you made the money disappear. It was all you, Mike."

"I had nothing to do with that," Mike said.

"Right. You're totally and completely innocent."

"I mean, about the money thing. I heard about it—everyone heard about it—but that wasn't my team. I don't know where you're getting your information from, but you got it wrong."

"He's right," said a voice behind me. Charlie's voice. "You've got it wrong. Mike wasn't on my team."

"But you said—"

"I didn't say who it was."

I suddenly pictured myself as Aunt Ginny. For sure, I felt like steam was coming out of my ears. "So who then?"

"Maddy. It was Maddy."

"Great. You see? Your information sucks!" Mike swung around to Madison. "Give me my jacket." Without waiting for her to answer, he wrenched open her locker door and grabbed it.

"No!" She got hold of one arm of the jacket and pulled. Mike yanked hard, and I heard something rip. Mike went flying backward into the locker behind him, dropping his part of the jacket. He stared at it in disbelief. Something fell out of the pocket, bounced and landed at my feet. I bent down and picked it up.

It was a brass with a horse in the middle of it and bells around the edges.

"Hey!" Mike grabbed it from my hand and examined it. "Where did you get this?"

"It fell out of your jacket."

"No way! No way! The last time I saw this, it was in the barn."

"Until you took it that night," I said.

"I didn't take anything, I wasn't there!" He spun around and stared at Maddy, who was holding the other part of the jacket.

You know how, in cartoons, when a character has a great idea or an inspiration, you see a lightbulb flash over their head? Well, that actually happened to me, and almost blinded me.

"I think the real question is, where did Madison get it?" I said. "She's the only other person who's been wearing your jacket."

We all turned to look at her.

Mike held up the brass. "Where did you get this, Maddy?"

Madison cowered. "Don't be mad at me, Mike. I was just trying to help you."

"By doing what?" Mike wasn't even trying to be nice. "Where did you get this brass?"

"I know how much you like them, Mike." Madison's eyes filled with tears. "I was just trying to help you."

Mike, Taylor and Charlie were silent.

"You were there the night of the fire, weren't you, Maddy?" I asked.

"No."

"The fire marshal said there were two flashlights as well as a kerosene lantern near the source of the fire. They've already fingerprinted them. Mr. Goran's fingerprints were on both of the flashlights but not on the lantern. There are other fingerprints on one of the flashlights, but they're guessing they're from a family member or maybe even Mike's grandfather. But I think all they have to do is fingerprint you to find out whose prints those are."

There was something else. "When you offered to alibi Mike, I thought you were trying to protect him. But you weren't. You were trying to protect yourself— because you knew you'd left your flashlight in there, and you didn't have an alibi."

"No. You're wrong."

"Where are the brasses, Madison?" I asked.

"Yeah, Maddy, where are they?" Mike stepped in closer to her. "Tell me."

"I was just helping you. That's all."

Taylor had reached into her pocket and was taking out her phone. My guess? She was about to call her dad. Let her.

"Where are the brasses, Maddy?" Mike's tone was gentler this time, coaxing.

Maddy opened her locker slowly. She bent down and lifted out a heavy burlap sack, which she handed to Mike. It jangled when Mike set it down on the concrete floor to open it.

It was full of brasses.

Horse brasses.

Mike looked up at Madison.

Tears dribbled down her cheeks. "I didn't mean for anyone to get hurt."

"What happened, Maddy?" I asked.

She cried silently.

"I know you took them the day of the fire," I said. "And I bet your fingerprints are all over the second flashlight in the barn. What happened? Did you set the fire on purpose?"

"No!" She looked horrified. "It was an accident. I swear. I snuck in through some loose boards."

I'd seen those boards. Mr. Goran had been planning to fix them before an unwanted animal got in. Madison had wriggled in instead. Mike never would have been able to manage.

"My flashlight conked out on me, but there was a lantern, so I lit it. I—" Her lip trembled again. "I finished collecting the brasses and I was getting down when I knocked over the lantern. It was an accident. Everything happened so fast after that. I looked for something to put out the fire with, but there wasn't anything. And it spread fast. So I ran. I just ran."

"What about Mr. Goran?"

"I didn't see him. I didn't know he was in the barn." She looked imploringly at Mike. "I know how important these are to you. I just wanted to help you."

Mike stood up. His face was impassive.

"You're going to have to tell the police what happened, Maddy," I said.

She shook her head. "It was an accident."

"You still have to tell them."

She was still shaking her head. "I did it for you, Mike."

Mike looked down at the brasses. Then, slowly, he turned and walked out of the locker room.

"Mike! Mike!" Maddy cried.

I glanced at Taylor.

"My dad's on his way," she said.

A car turned in to our driveway a week later. It was Aram. He walked around the side of our house to the kitchen door at the back.

"Anyone home?" he called through the screen, one arm behind his back.

"You're back!" I was so glad to see him.

"Back to stay," he said when I opened the door for him. "It's going to take a while for my things to get here from Afghanistan. But it looks like this is going to be my home until my father is able to make some decisions."

Mr. Goran had regained consciousness, but he was still in the hospital. He was going to need several operations once he was well enough. The burns were the worst on his arms, but his doctor was optimistic that given time, and barring infection, he would recover enough to be able to go home. Aram had resigned his position with the international aid agency. He was going to run the farm as best he could while his father recovered. After that, well, "we'll see when we see," he said. "How is that girl? Madison?"

I had to tell him I didn't know much, only that she'd been arrested for breaking into the barn and that no charges had been laid for the fire. She hadn't meant for it to start. It was an accident, after all. I hadn't seen or talked to her since the confrontation in the locker room at the park.

"Riley, do you—oh." Aunt Ginny had a towel around her wet hair and was wearing bunny slippers when she came into the kitchen. She stopped short when she saw we had company. Her face turned scarlet. She scurried away. A moment later she was back, her hair damp but combed out. "Aram," she said. "Good to see you. You'll stay for supper, I hope. Riley made fried chicken."

Aram smiled. "I'd be delighted." From behind his back he produced a bouquet of flowers, which he presented to Aunt Ginny. "And tomorrow night, I'd like to take you two out to dinner—to thank you for everything you've done for my father and me."

I heard my ringtone and reached for my phone. It was Charlie.

"Everything's almost ready, Aunt Ginny," I said. "You just have to let the chicken drain for a few minutes." I headed for the stairs.

"Where are you going?" Aunt Ginny asked.

"To a movie. With Charlie and Ashleigh." With my new friends. Maybe this place wasn't going to be so bad after all.

NORAH McCLINTOCK won the Crime Writers of Canada's Arthur Ellis Award for crime fiction for young people five times. She wrote more than sixty YA novels, including two other Riley Donovan books, and contributed to The Seven Prequels, Seven (the series), the Seven Sequels and the Secrets series.